AMANDA

A Sweet Romantic Comedy

SARAH MONZON

RADIANT PUBLICATIONS

1

AMANDA

*W*hoever said "It's better to have loved and lost than never to have loved at all" was the biggest liar in Earth's history. I'm talking right up there with the serpent in the garden of Eden. That's how much hogwash that pretty piece of fruit dangled before all our broken hearts is. Because how is it ever better to live without love when you've experienced it in its truest form?

I let my head fall to my desk, moving my arms at the last second to cushion the blow. Although, maybe I should have let my brow take the full brunt of tender flesh against unforgiving wood. The abuse would be no less than I deserved, according to some.

I'd seen the judgment in my coworkers' eyes as I'd taken my box of shame—the one the division had given me to move my belongings out of my closet-sized office—and carried the white cardboard cube to the elevator. I hadn't been fired. Not exactly. But my boss had been less than impressed with my firefighting skills. More specifically, that I hadn't been able to put out the flames the Stampeders' starting pitcher had ignited when he took a knee during the national anthem. Because of that, they'd transferred me to the other team bazillionaire Jordan Phillips owned. The *football* team.

No, the irony was not lost on me.

I lifted my head and blinked up at the computer screen, a groan lodged in my throat.

The prospect of working with the San Diego Condors had sounded like a nice change of pace.

At first.

I preferred football to baseball for one. The Condors were also having a great season and even had a chance at the Super Bowl this year. And to top it all off, I could take Nicole's daughter, Sierra, to a game. She played quarterback for a youth team and had a killer arm. A few pictures of her beaming face in the team's colors of burgundy and navy plus a signed ball from Grant Hawthorne would earn me brownie points with my friends to make up for all the times I'd had to cancel plans with them lately.

There was just one snag in the whole deal. One hiccup. One...well...one Peter Reynolds, defensive end.

My breath shuttered in my lungs.

But how hard could avoiding a six-foot-four, 260-

pound man be? Especially when I was probably the last person on the planet he'd ever want to see.

I scanned the words in the email for the third time, willing the letters to somehow rearrange themselves to say something else. Anything else.

Amanda,

We need you to work your magic. Peter Reynolds has gotten some spotlight lately for his sportsman-like conduct on and off the field, and we want you to make sure his name continues to trend as we head toward the playoffs. Drop everything else. Peter Reynolds is your only focus.

Jim

That *focus* blurred my surroundings, fogging the photo beside my computer—one of my sewing circle friends and me at Molly's wedding, striking poses like we were the lost members of Charlie's Angels, finger pistols and all—into an indecipherable haze.

What would that person with the oh-so-helpful love/loss platitude say to me in this situation? Probably something equally unhelpful.

Or maybe they'd adopt one of my coworkers' expressions. One that says it's all my fault. But that's only partly true. Had the decision been mine alone five years ago, things would be different right now. For one,

I wouldn't be slumping in my cheap office chair, wishing floors literally opened up and swallowed people. New low, wanting the fate of Korah.

But I hadn't been able to make my own decisions for so long I'd almost forgotten what it was like. Instead of being my own woman, I had to continually bend to Delores's will. *She* was why I cancelled my plans so often that my friends thought I was a flake. *She* was why I'd been pushing my boss to allow me to work from home for so long. And *she* was why I'd broken both my and Peter Reynolds's hearts our freshman year at the University of Florida (Go Gators!).

The logical thing would be for me to separate myself from Delores, as she was obviously not a healthy influence on my life.

Ha. Pun not intended.

See, while Delores was all too real, no one could see her. No, she wasn't an imaginary friend. Ana had been the last friend that only I could see, and that friendship had ended when I was five. Delores wasn't imaginary; she was invisible. And yes, there was a difference— even if I had been told by multiple people that everything was only in my head. But just because something is invisible, doesn't mean it's not real. And since the many doctors I'd seen couldn't diagnose me and give this thing that had taken over my body a name, I'd done it for them.

That wasn't right. They'd attempted and failed to name it. Lupus. Sjögren's syndrome. Polymyalgia rheumatica. But none of those were right, so Delores she remained—both in name and in my body. An unwanted controlling guest I couldn't kick out.

I clicked out of the email and brought up the Condors' roster. As the team's social media manager, I had most of the information memorized and turned into hashtags, although I'd developed a habit of quickly scrolling past a certain defensive lineman.

His picture brought back too many memories. Lazily tubing down the Ichetucknee River hand in hand. Making out under the stars in the back of his pickup after the football games. The devastation in his eyes when I told him it was over between us.

You did the right thing, I told myself for the millionth time since that day. After all, didn't someone once say that if you loved someone, you had to let them go?

My finger rolled over my mouse. I should probably stop listening to all these sayings. If they were written to make people feel better, then they were failing miserably.

My hand lifted, hovering over the mouse. The screen filled with a familiar face. Hazel eyes stared back at me, a kaleidoscope of greens, golds, and browns. He must have been in a good mood when the picture was taken. Emerald green dominated his irises, flecks of gold glittered like the sun's rays, and a rim of brown had been relegated to the borders. When he was angry, that brown would bleed center, like thunder clouds rolling in and blocking out the warmth.

My favorite interplay of colors, though, had been the way his eyes looked when he gazed at me. Before I broke his heart. Before I stole the light out of them.

At one point, I'd have sworn they danced. It was like the clearest day in the forest, when a breeze would move along the branches and send leaves to twirling, reflecting light streaming down from above. When he looked at me with that expression—

I minimized my browser and let my head fall back. My cheeks felt flushed and my skin warm—a toss-up between Peter's lingering effect on me and Delores's punctuality at turning up my body temperature. Clocks could be set to my afternoon fevers.

A dull knock sounded against the flimsy partition of my cubicle. I lifted my head and tried to ignore the pinch at the base of my skull.

Jim stood on the other side of the half wall. Unlike a lot of the other bosses, he didn't sport a suit but had on a pair of jeans and a jersey. He probably had more Condors memorabilia than the pro shop.

"You got my email?" he asked. That was Jim, right to the point. No use for any preambles.

I massaged my fingers under my small desk. "About that. Not that I'm ungrateful for this opportunity here, but have you talked to Peter about this?"

Unless he'd changed, Peter tried to live a quiet life. Well, as quiet as an NFL player's life could be. I had it on good authority that his social media accounts were managed in house instead of personally, one reason he had the least followers and engagement out of everyone on the team. Even those who weren't starters.

And if he knew I'd be the one heading up this project...

Jim held up his hand. "I admit he was hesitant when I first brought up the angle of using him to keep the team's name in the limelight, but he came around to my way of thinking. I assured him you were more than capable—"

"You mentioned me?" My voice squeaked.

Jim's brows furrowed. "Why wouldn't I? Anyway, as I was saying, I assured him you—"

"And he didn't refuse on the spot? After you told him he'd be working with me?" My heart raced. *Delores, is that you? Knock it off. I'm kind of already having a crisis here.*

"No." Jim crossed his arms, his frustration at my interruptions evident. "Actually, that was about the time he seemed to be swayed. Either way, he's on board." My boss lowered his arms and pinned me with a look I'd seen him use on aggressive journalists. "You know our expectations." He might as well have tacked on a *don't screw this up.* "Reynolds is waiting in the conference room now."

"Now?" The octave of my voice could rival a Chipette.

Jim gripped the top of the partition. "You're acting weird. Stop it. And get your butt to the conference room and our boy trending on social media." He left without another word.

Brain fog often made it difficult for me to gather my thoughts. Now they fled me as if they were playing hide-and-seek in a mist-shrouded San Francisco Bay that managed to conceal even the Golden Gate Bridge.

Peter knew we would be working together. He hadn't refused or run the other way. Why?

You know why.

A memory flashed in my mind. Peter's head bent, forehead resting on mine. His big hands warm against the small of my back, cradling me inside the wall of his arms, his deep voice whispering, "I'll always love you."

"No." My spoken words shattered the image. He couldn't... He wouldn't... "He can't."

My hands shook as I rose, knowing I couldn't blame Delores this time. I lifted my fingers and touched the messy bun on top of my head. Five days of dry shampoo couldn't combat the greasy build up any longer, so I'd gathered my long brown tresses and secured them in the best way possible to hide my hygiene abuse. Delores didn't like showers, and she often protested for hours after I took one. Better to look a bit unkempt than deal with her temper tantrum.

Most women would want to look their best when they knew they were about to walk into a room where their ex waited for them. High heels to make their legs look great. Maybe a silk blouse to make them feel great. Female armor. I looked down at my tennis shoes with the Dr. Scholl's inserts inside and let my gaze trail over my pleated skirt with mustard stain and my white polyester top with crescent sweat stains under my arms.

Maybe the grunge look was my own sort of armor. Even though there was no way Peter was still in love with me, the way I looked wouldn't turn any heads. Besides, I didn't want to make him fall in love with me again, so the outfit and dirty hair worked.

Okay, that wasn't entirely true. Because no matter that I'd ended our relationship years ago, Peter still held my heart. Unfortunately, Delores still controlled my body.

None of the reasons for giving him up in the first place had changed. I couldn't be the anvil tethering down his rising star. So no matter how sweet or charming Peter could be, I absolutely could not let the best defensive end in the National Football League tackle my resolve.

Things had to remain professional between us.

They just had to.

@AmandaMurphy

If you had one do-over in life, what would it be? #GoBackInTime

#DoItAgain #MakeAChange

2

PETER

*M*y leg bounced under the solid mahogany conference table, the heel of my shoe ticking away the seconds like a silent clock hand. I hated waiting. Waiting was too passive. Too much like being benched in life. I'd rather *do* something than cool my heels waiting for the next play to come to me.

The lacquered top of the table cooled my palms as I pushed up to stand, then I strode to the refreshment cart near the back of the room. A clear glass pitcher sweated condensation, the ice tinkling when I tilted the mouth to pour a cup of water.

Somewhere on this floor, behind one of the doors or sequestered within the half walls of the cubicles, sat Amanda Murphy. I could go charging down the halls like a bull in a china shop looking for her, or I could wait here until she eventually came to me.

I lifted the glass to my lips, downing the contents in one gulp.

How many times had I pictured it? Amanda returning. Apologizing. Saying she'd been wrong that day. That she'd do anything for another chance at the future we'd planned to have together.

A day passed. No knock on my door. No tear-stained girl on my porch to wrap in my arms. The days turned into weeks. Still I waited, expecting she'd turn up. That the constant ache in my chest from her absence would finally release when our eyes met.

But then the weeks had turned into years, and I'd finally had to face the facts. She wasn't coming back. The girl I loved didn't love me in return.

I would have continued to believe that lie if it hadn't been for her roommate and a drunken confession. The team had thrown a party after a big win—not my scene, but I'd been pulled along against my will. When I spotted Morgan in the press of bodies, red solo cup in her hand, I thought to give her space. Avoid the inevitable memories she brought with her.

But then I noticed the person next to her, his large hand clasping her small wrist as he dragged her to a back room. My long legs ate up the distance separating us, and I was able to step between them, taking the hit he'd meant for her.

Later, after I bundled her in my truck to take her home, she rested her head against the glass of the passenger window and called me a martyr, just like

Amanda. Instead of correcting her on the first part, I honed in on the second. I asked her what she meant. She swore me to secrecy, the alcohol making her forget Amanda had probably meant to keep this information from me forever. I wrapped my pinkie around hers, and my universe shifted.

I went from confused heartbreak to raging mad in the time it took to lunge across the line of scrimmage.

Amanda may have claimed selflessness, but I'd never heard of anything more self*ish*. Not to mention controlling, conniving, and more than a little insulting. In a single act, she'd stolen one of the most important decisions from me and judged my character lacking.

I'd long ago assumed that was the end of it. She'd chosen her path (and mine) and we'd gone our separate ways. Imagine my surprise when life handed me a gotcha moment.

First off, I hadn't asked for all the publicity the sports channels and journalists were throwing my way. I played the game to the best of my ability and adhered to the philosophy I tried to model on the field but which applied off as well: when someone is knocked down, you offer them a helping hand up. Never mind the pesky detail that I'd been the one to knock him— usually the quarterback—down in the first place.

But the fact that breaking the record for the most sacks grew more tangible every game, coupled with my sportsmanlike conduct of helping pick quarterbacks up off the ground, had garnered me more attention than

I'd ever thought I'd have. Besides superfans and those who played fantasy football, the names of defensive players didn't get the same amount of air time as, say, Tom Brady or Ezekiel Elliott—the ones putting points up on the scoreboard.

But a few highlights on ESPN and some reminders of my record from the announcers had piqued the ears of the Condors' franchise bigwigs. They liked the air time and would milk me and my plays for all we were worth. Hopefully they'd remember that worth come contract negotiations.

At first, I hadn't been too keen on the idea. Besides recently, I'd managed to keep my head down and fly under the radar. Being recognized in public was still a rare occurrence unless the PR team had rustled up coverage for a particular event. My private life was still that.

I'd appeased the powers that be by allowing them to set up social media accounts for me, though I'd yet to post anything on one personally. Showing up on people's TVs on Sundays and an occasional Monday or Thursday gave some a sense of entitlement when it came to my personal life. I didn't relish the idea of opening that door further by throwing out a welcome mat on Instagram or Facebook.

I still wasn't thrilled, but it had been a losing battle. The determined set to Jim's jaw had said as much. When he looked something up on his phone and slid the device over to me, I stopped listening all together.

The girl of my memories, who had turned into the woman that sometimes haunted my dreams, grinned up at me in HD resolution.

Had there been an official in the room, I'd have demanded he throw the yellow flag to signal a foul. Gazing down at Amanda's photo had been more than an interference—it was enough to take me out of the game. But I'd eventually managed to shake myself off and notice details I'd missed because of the brightness of her smile.

She'd grown out her hair. The edges no longer teased her shoulders but hung in long dark waves to what seemed like halfway down her back. While her smile gave off manufactured light, her glacier-blue eyes were veiled. Tightness pinched the corners of her mouth. A mask of carefree joy to hide a secret she shared with no one.

Photo after photo painted the same picture. No cares. No worries. No struggle. Only success and poise and a life to envy. I had to wonder what more she hid. When the selfie smile turned off and the likes and comments vanished under a pile of endless newsfeed, what was her life really like?

The turn of the doorknob sounded behind me, and I slowly pivoted, shoving my hands in the front pockets of my dress pants. They sometimes had a mind of their own, and I wasn't sure if, upon seeing Amanda for the first time since she'd dumped me, they'd want to strangle her, hug her, or roll her up like a burrito with bubble wrap.

Like a video editing effect, the door opened in slow motion. I forced my shoulders to relax and wiped my face of the confused feelings conjured by the anticipation of seeing Amanda again.

The top of her head came into view first, her face parallel to the floor. The swirl pattern in the industrial carpeting wasn't interesting enough to elicit that type of concentration. One corner of my lip curved in satisfaction. As much as I'd never expected to see Amanda again, *her* surprise and discomfort at meeting me face-to-face after she'd written me off would be tenfold.

I leaned back, adopting an unaffected stance, and waited. A small part of me itched to step forward. To do something to ease the hunch of her shoulders and lighten her distress, but I reined that part in.

She shut the door behind her but still didn't lift her face. I took the opportunity to study her. Her hair looked like a ball of yarn that a cat had played with, all piled messily on top of her head. Her clothes fit her form in a way that made my mouth go dry, making me push my hands deeper into my pockets.

Someone could argue the pictures she shared online painted her in a better light, but given the option, I'd always find her more beautiful like this. Unfiltered. Real.

Tension grew in the space between us, the silence expanding with every second until it filled the room.

Slowly she lifted her chin, her wary eyes coming to rest on me.

I stared back, waiting. She'd had the last word before; only right she had the first now. Her gaze flicked away, and her tongue darted out to lick chapped lips. Only the self-control built over years of a disciplined life kept my eyes focused on hers instead of dipping down to follow the movement at her mouth.

She looked back at me before her gaze skittered again. Her hand rose to touch her temple. "Is it hot in here, or is it just me?"

I shrugged. The heat had kicked on when Jim escorted me to the conference room. Winter in San Diego didn't require any crazy-type snow gear. It wasn't uncommon to still see people walking around in shorts and sandals, even though the weather had turned with a seasonal chill, dipping into the sixties. But no, the room wouldn't make anyone want to dash to the thermostat.

"Maybe I'll just..." She pointed to the ice water on the refreshment cart behind me.

A small part of me perked, prodding me to turn and pour her a glass of water. I ignored that voice, keeping my face placid.

She shuffled forward, walking in an arc instead of a straight line to keep as much space between us as possible. But with a large table eating up more than just the middle of the room, plus the oversized chairs on the wings, she had to shift at an angle to get around me without brushing against my front.

With anyone else, I would have moved. I wasn't normally a rude person and was kind of ashamed of how I was acting. Still, my feet remained planted. My chest might even have puffed out, shrinking the miniscule gap between our bodies.

Faint undertones of spun sugar wafted around Amanda, pulling at both my memory and the corners of my lips. I'd forgotten her affinity for cotton candy-scented body spray and the way she smelled faintly of the county fair after she'd spritzed herself.

Ice clinked against the glass as she lifted the pitcher. Her hand shook, chipping away at my resolve to maintain an unaffected front. With a huff, I mobilized my body, which had been statuesque until then, and covered her hand with my own.

Her breath sucked through her teeth. Someone pushed pause on the room, and we both stilled. This time, when her eyes met mine, they held. *What are you doing?* they seemed to ask.

I didn't know. Not a single, solitary clear thought had entered my head since she'd stepped foot through the doorway.

Her fingers moved under mine, but instead of loosening my grip so she could pull her hand free, I firmed my grasp.

This time the air through her teeth sounded like a hiss, and I immediately dropped my hand. "Are you okay?" My question came out gruff, hiding my genuine concern.

Her eyes cooled to their glacier blue. "I'm fine, you oaf, despite your manhandling." She poured the water and took a sip.

I leaned down and purred in her ear, "I think you've forgotten how gentle I can be." My breath made a wisp of hair at her nape dance along her neck. Her shoulders shook in a shudder, and I straightened with satisfaction.

She pivoted on her heel, then rose up to her toes. Cute that she thought those extra inches would add any sort of intimidation to her glare.

"If we're going to do this, then we need to have some rules in place."

"What do you mean *if?*"

She blinked. "What do you mean what do I mean?"

I shrugged and dug my hands back into my pockets. "The way I see it, neither of us has much of a choice here. The franchise wants me to be more active in the virtual world, and they've assigned you the job of seeing that happen." I shrugged again. "So sorry, but I see no reason to negotiate terms and conditions."

She gritted her teeth. "Fine." With a flourish of her arm, she gestured toward the table. "Should we at least sit to discuss a game plan?"

I pulled out a chair and sat. "Sounds good, but before we get to that, I've been wanting to ask you something."

Amanda crossed her legs. "What's that?" She took another sip of her water.

"How's Delores?"

@CondorsOfficial

Your feel-good story of the day. <3 @JebAbeson surprised a north county athlete with cerebral palsy with new adaptive sports equipment.

3

AMANDA

*L*ungs do not like to inhale water. Pretty elementary stuff, but as soon as Peter mentioned Delores, I sucked in a sharp breath. Problem was, I was also taking a drink.

Must—*hack, hack, hack*—not—*cough, cough*—drown —*wheeze, hack, cough.*

Not that anyone had ever died from a sip of water going down the wrong pipe, but the way my body spasmed and convulsed to expel the intruding liquid, I was in danger of popping a blood vessel or having a brain aneurysm or something. Maybe. Probably. Honestly, my medical expertise came from WebMD and centered around autoimmune disorders.

My eyes glazed over as I fought for a full, clear breath. The sound of a chair scraping the floor was almost drowned out by all my racket.

Large, strong fingers encircled my wrists, lifting my

hands in the air over my head and shaking them in small motions side to side. My arms jiggled like limp noodles, the flabby skin where triceps should be waving like flags of surrender.

I sucked in another breath and coughed some more. Blinked past the moisture gathering in my eyes and caught my reflection in the large mirror hanging on the opposite wall.

Hands limp over my head, arms akimbo, and face red, I looked like one of the orangutans they had at the zoo. If only I could find some tree limbs and swing away in retreat.

I attempted another breath and felt my lungs expand. The ache lessened and oxygen moved more freely. After a few more small coughs, everything returned to normal.

"Better?" Peter asked, letting my arms fall to my sides.

I swallowed, throat a little raw, but tilted my chin in a show of pride. *Show* being the pivotal word. Any amount of dignity I'd possessed had been thrown out the window long ago. "Yes, thank you. Although, what was with the lifting my hands over my head thing?"

He lowered himself back into his seat. "Thought I heard somewhere that it was supposed to help. Normally I'd just thump someone on the back, but..."

His sentence dangled as he gave me a direct look—one that searched to make sure I was okay while simultaneously accusing me that I wasn't.

What did he know? Wait. I didn't want that question answered. Although, he *had* asked about Delores. Specifically. By name.

Maybe there had been a mutual acquaintance at U of F with the same name? A co-ed from Intro to Psych or perhaps one of the girls who liked to hook up with the football team.

Or maybe I could use the whole coughing fit as a perfect diversion, and Peter wouldn't ever remember he'd posed a question in the first place.

I scraped at the last dregs of my energy and pushed my shoulders back. I felt like I'd been run over by a Mack truck, and all I wanted to do was crawl into bed and pull the covers over my head. I also didn't want Peter to remember whatever he thought he knew about a certain someone.

No one ever really believed I was sick anyway, so kicking him off that train shouldn't be that hard.

"We should start by downloading the apps to your phone. Jim specifically mentioned Twitter and Instagram, but there are a lot more platforms you could choose from if you wanted." I held out my hand for his phone. I could walk him through the process of the app store, but getting everything set up with the accounts already in place would go faster if I stayed at the helm.

He pulled his phone out of his pocket—an outdated model with a cracked screen that made my fingers twitch and my mind jump to reasons someone making NFL dollars would be carrying around such a beat-up relic—and set it on the table, his palm covering the top, barring me from the device.

He held his phone hostage and, somehow, I knew what the ransom would be.

"Delores?" he asked again, an almost-challenging edge to his normally kind timbre.

I tilted my head, pretending to remember whoever this mystery woman was. "Delores…" I tapped my chin, then widened my eyes. "Was she the blonde in Poli-Sci who always asked to borrow our notes? Sorry. I haven't really kept in touch with anyone from freshman year."

"I'm aware," he said dryly. "And you know that's not who I'm referring to."

I inched my fingers toward his imprisoned phone. Could I execute a phone jailbreak before Peter caught on to me? Probably not. "Now that we've figured that out…" I pointed to his cell.

He smirked. "Nice try." He waited, that faint smile freezing, then melting from his face the longer I sat in silence.

His hazel eyes morphed in front of mine, the brown hue invading the green. He sighed, pocketing his phone. "I guess that's it then." His sad gaze swept over me, almost as if he were cataloguing my features. He stood, moving toward the door.

"Where are you going?" I could've kicked myself at the panic in my voice. But if Peter walked out the door, I might as well follow him—with all my things and a fresh copy of my resumé. No way I'd be shifted into another position after two failures. Jobs weren't like baseball; I wouldn't get a third chance before I struck out.

He paused, shoving his hands into the pockets of his dress pants. His arms flexed, pulling against the fabric of his checkered button-up. Journalists, both those of reputable publications and not, loitered around the premises. Most of the players tried to keep a clean reputation, and dressing nicely went a long way to prejudice fans toward them in a positive light. But when part of Peter's job was pumping iron so he could drive full-grown athletic guys into the ground, the circumference of the sleeve of a dress shirt probably felt a bit like a corset for his biceps.

That was the only reason why I stared at the thickness of his arm. Honest.

"Amanda."

I dragged my gaze up.

Dark green flecks emerged from the brown dominating his irises. "All of you are expecting me to open up my private life to potentially millions of people." He held up his hand when I made to interject. "I'm not so out-of-the-know with social media that I don't understand how it works. If the franchise was satisfied with just sharing about my life on the field, then they'd be happy keeping the status quo and letting one of the PR interns come up with posts. But they're not. They want fans to have glimpses into how I live outside the endzones. Millions of people." He shifted over his feet. "I'm asking you to let in one person. Me."

I hadn't always been so closed off about my health struggles. Even Peter, if he thought far enough back, would remember an increase in doctor's visits. But he'd probably forgotten, because the doctors had never been able to find anything wrong with me. It wasn't like I'd come back from a visit and announced I had cancer. Saying those words, receiving that diagnosis, was life changing. And not just for the person fighting the disease. Cancer. It was...it was defining.

What a weird thing to be almost envious of, I know. But five and a half years down my own health journey and I still had no definition. Not only that, but those who'd supported me at the beginning had long ago fallen away. After so many times of doctors saying they couldn't find anything wrong with me, my friends started to believe the professionals. I couldn't blame them. They couldn't feel the constant pain that went bone deep or the sloughing weariness that zapped my energy. They couldn't see the brain fog or the tingling or the numbness. On the outside, I didn't look sick, so to them, that mean I must not be.

After a while, continually hearing friends and specialists say my symptoms were all in my head had made me begin to wonder if it weren't true. In a moment of clarity, I'd realized I was too tired. I didn't have the energy to face my sickness every day and try to convince people who'd claimed to love me that something was really wrong. So instead of fighting, I gave in. Delores became my little secret. My private battle. If no one knew about her, then I wouldn't have to deal with the disappointment of watching my friends and family lose faith in me. Life was better that way.

Which begged the question...

"How do you know about Delores?" I tried to keep my voice casual. I really did, but there was a reason I never played poker with any of the guys from work. (The fact I got a full house and a royal flush confused was only a small part of it.) If I had good cards—at least, what I *thought* were good—I had a hard time not smiling. I also couldn't bluff to save my soul.

I expected a flash of victory to cross Peter's face, but unlike me, he knew how to play the game. Funny how I'd forgotten that.

"Morgan told me."

"My old roommate? When did you run into her?" *And why were you guys talking about me?*

"It was at a party a few years back."

Nothing like a college party to reveal one's drunken condition. Or that of one's cells and proteins. Mine seemed to function about as well as someone who'd taken a dozen shots of Jose Cuervo on an empty stomach.

"What did she tell you?" A good poker player could guess their opponent's hand. If only I were slightly better than abysmal at the game.

Peter pulled his chair back out and sat, his body facing me full on. He'd always been good at that. Direct focus.

My skin flushed. I wanted to blame Delores, but this response was all on Peter. He'd always had this effect on me.

"Doesn't matter what she told me. I want to hear it from you."

This was me folding. Pushing all my chips his direction. I sighed and let my shoulders round. "I have an undiagnosed autoimmune disorder. The doctors haven't figured out what's wrong with me or how to help me feel better."

I looked up at him, expecting to see pity. Maybe a little sympathy. Worst case, a twinge of disbelief. Good thing the bets were off. Guess Peter hadn't gotten the memo that I'd conceded defeat, because his face remained as unmoving as a stone cliff.

My heart fell a bit in my chest, my ribs aching to hold it in place. I should feel vindicated. Hadn't he just proven my position on not letting anyone in? Still, it hurt more than I'd thought it would.

"Right. Phone?"

He ignored my outstretched hand. "Who knows?"

"What do you mean?"

The muscles in his jaw pulsed. "I mean, was I the only one you cut out of your life and hid this from or —" He shook his head, a self-deprecating laugh slipping past his lips. "Actually, no, that's not what I mean."

After a deep breath he started again. "I just..." He groaned. "Amanda, do you have a support system, or are you being your typical stubborn self and trying to do this all alone?"

My head knocked back. "What do you mean 'my typical stubborn self'?"

Yes, I added air quotes.

He laughed. Threw his head back and full-on belly laughed.

If I were really from the South, I'd have said, *Well, I never,* in the most politely offended voice imaginable. As I was originally from the Midwest, I just rolled my eyes.

Once he got over whatever it was he'd thought so funny, he looked at me. "I think we can stop with all these 'What do you mean?'s. You and I both know *exactly* what the other is thinking. We always have."

He paused.

My brain supplied, *We always will.* I looked away from him, but not quickly enough. His knowing gaze said he'd thought the same thing and knew I had too.

This really wasn't how this meeting was supposed to go. I'd broken Peter's heart. He was supposed to be mad at me, not rewiring our brain wavelengths so they were set to the same frequency again. An angry Peter would be a safe Peter. I needed him to want to keep his distance. This...concern he exhibited made me nervous. I didn't like it.

"Look, I have my reasons. I don't need to explain

myself to you." I winced for him as he still sat like The Rock from the Fantastic Four.

"I'll take that as you being your stubborn self."

What he called stubbornness, I called self-preservation. "Whatever, just don't go telling anyone, okay?"

Peter suddenly found the painting of Super Bowl I hanging behind me extremely fascinating.

"Peter."

No response.

"Peter."

His body may as well have been switched for a wax model.

"Peter!"

His eyes shifted to land on mine. "Fine. I won't tell. On one condition."

I'd have gritted my teeth if I hadn't thought the action would make my headache worse. "What might that be?"

He shrugged as if my whole life didn't depend on the next words coming out of his mouth. "I haven't decided yet."

@AmandaMurphy

I need a new show to watch on #Netflix. What are you currently bingeing?

4

PETER

*S*imon and Garfunkel crooned through my speakers, proclaiming to be a rock and an island. I snorted, letting one hand fall from the steering wheel to punch the radio dial. I'd had enough islanders for one day. Amanda might as well have erected a neon no-trespassing sign visible from the International Space Station and planted deep-sea bombs to explode if anyone ever tried to get too close.

I didn't understand her reasoning—not that she'd bothered to explain it to me anyway. Not five years ago and not today. But I didn't get it. When I was sick, which thankfully didn't happen often, I was a bit of a baby. Not so much with injuries, as those came with the athletic territory, but flu and seasonal colds kicked my butt. I still played (I wasn't a *real* baby), but I moaned and complained and milked any sort of sympathy for all it was worth. (Look at me being more self-aware than the rest of the male population. They were all babies too. They just wouldn't admit it.)

But why didn't Amanda want a support system? Why did she think shutting out everyone who'd ever cared for her was a good idea?

I shoved my truck into park and let my head fall back on the seat rest. Why was I allowing myself to care so much? Amanda and her decisions no longer concerned me—she'd made sure of that. But there I was, like an idiot, trying to figure out the best way to build a bridge to the stupid island she'd sequestered herself on.

I should walk away. Or sprint like I'd caught an interception and had a running back hot on my heels. She didn't want me in her life; she'd made that abundantly clear. But the thought of leaving things how they were and not doing something seemed wrong on so many levels, and I couldn't take that first step away from her.

I groaned and slipped my phone out of my pocket. Two new apps cluttered my home screen. I bypassed them to open my web browser. Her condition not having a name made searching symptoms more difficult. Of course, if Miss Stubborn Pants would just tell me herself, then I wouldn't have to guess. But that would be too easy.

I typed in autoimmune disorder symptoms, and the page loaded. Right on top: *Symptoms vary widely based on the type of autoimmune disease.*

Great. Super helpful.

I scrolled down and found a general list including fatigue, achy muscles, swelling, numbness, hair loss, low-grade fevers, and on it went. I continued reading. "Autoimmune disorders occur when the immune system attacks and damages the body's healthy tissue." Some type of bodily civil war then?

Tap. Tap. Tap.

I lifted my head and looked out the window.

Trey stood there, chin cocked to the side and a football wedged between his inner forearm and hip. "Are you coming or what, man?"

I pushed the button on the side of my phone to lock the screen, and it went black. Reaching for the handle on the door's inner panel, I pulled then stepped out. "I'm coming. Don't get your panties in a wad."

A year ago, Trey would've been ready to go to blows after a comment like that. Now he just shook his head at me and how lame he thought I sounded.

"Bruh, the only one of us wearin' panties is you. My mama could've made that tackle against Aaron Jones last week with one hand tied behind her back, but you let him juke you." He tossed the football between his hands. "You should be embarrassed, bruh."

A grin stretched across my face. Aaron Jones was at the top of his game and had slipped past me because of his skill. Trey would only call me out for one reason. "Lost to Miguel in fantasy football again?"

"Dude can't even catch a ball." His lips pulled to the side. "It ain't right."

I swung my arm over Trey's shoulders, waiting for the automatic stiffening and eventual relaxation. "My mama would've learned not to bet against a genius long ago."

He glared at me out of the corner of his eye, but the look didn't hold any heat.

"What were the stakes?" I asked.

"Bathroom duty for a week," he grumbled.

With eight teens living at Boys to Men—not to be confused with the R&B group—the bathrooms could get super nasty. I would know, as I'd cleaned them my fair share of times.

The chain-link fence clanked as we opened and then closed the gate, then crossed the asphalt track to the field in the middle. Miguel sat off to the side, a slouchy beanie on his head even though the sun beat down and the temperatures hovered in the pleasant range. The sun glared off the screen of the tablet he held in his hand.

I stopped beside the fifteen-year-old who had gotten in trouble for hacking and underage gambling. I wouldn't be surprised if the next time I showed up he was gone—recruited by some three-letter-acronym government agency. He had that level of skill.

"How are you doing, Miguel?"

He didn't bother looking up. Just kept tapping the screen. "Good."

"How's school?"

"Good."

"Want to join us on the field today?"

"Nope."

"Going to take over the world one day?"

No answer.

"Good talk. We should do it again sometime."

"Yep."

I grinned and jogged onto the field. Kids waited, some lounging on the grass while others bunched together talking.

Look for opportunities to snap pictures and create narratives about the ins and outs of your day. People know your public persona, but they use social media to get to know who you are off the field. Amanda's words rang in my ears.

Yeah, no. This time and these kids would never be an *opportunity* for me. Other players may ride the waves of public opinion after charity events, and of course we were all expected to give back to our communities— even giving out the Walter Payton NFL Man of the Year award in recognition of outstanding service—but I refused to use these kids or my connection to them to put myself forward in any way.

I'd have to figure out something else to post. Later. At the moment, I had a group of teen boys to torture. After drills, a scrimmage using flags instead of pads, and a killer motivational speech, if I said so myself, I told the kids to stay out of trouble and headed back to my truck.

Trey jogged to catch up with me. "Can I hitch a ride back to the house?"

"Sure." I glanced back to see if Miguel needed a ride too but didn't see his slouchy hat anywhere.

"He said he had to meet someone and would find his own way home," Trey supplied.

Suspicion arose at the vague *someone*. Overall, these were good kids who came from bad situations, but they'd also made not-so-great decisions. John, the guy who ran Boys to Men, did his best to guide the boys onto better paths toward brighter futures, but it wasn't always so easy to sever ties with the past or avoid slipping back into old ways.

"Dude, I don't think you need to worry. Not like he's gonna rob a bank or somethin'."

Maybe not at gunpoint, but I wouldn't put it past him to get over some firewall or whatever and transfer just the right amount of funds not to raise any red flags.

Trey sighed. "He's going to see his sister."

My hand paused halfway to the truck's handle. I pinned Trey with a look. "You know where?"

His jaw tightened. "I ain't no squealin' pig. I only told you that much so you wouldn't think he was doin' somethin' dumb."

If Miguel was going back to his old neighborhood, then that's exactly what I thought. Neither his brother nor his gang would react kindly to seeing Miguel after he'd rolled on them.

"You're not a snitch, Trey. You're a good friend. And friends have each other's backs." I opened the door and slid into the driver's seat while Trey got into the passenger seat. I waited. Given enough time, Trey would make the right decision. I hoped.

"Fine. But if we're doing some cop stake-out thing, I'm gonna need food."

I put the truck into gear. "Who said you were coming?"

He snorted. "You ain't goin' without me."

Without him, I wouldn't know exactly where Miguel was planning on meeting Camilla. Hopefully the kid had enough common sense to meet somewhere public and neutral.

I backed out of the parking lot and took a left. "In-N-Out sound good?"

As if anyone could turn down California's best fast-food hamburger.

A quick trip through the drive-thru, and the cab of the truck smelled of grilled beef patties and salty French fries.

Trey took a huge bite of his double-double. "They're meeting at the coffee shop on Ranchera and Third."

Not too far away, thankfully. After maneuvering through some back roads, I found a parking spot on the street one store down, then killed the engine. Everything seemed calm. Nothing out of the ordinary.

I held up the paper bag with the In-N-Out logo and

snapped a picture. Probably not what Amanda had in mind, but she'd have to deal.

"What was that?"

My head snapped up, thinking Trey had seen something suspicious, only to catch him staring at me with his eyebrows raised.

"Why'd you take a pic of the bag?"

"Oh. You know. Social media."

He shook his head. "Bruh, that's so lame."

Wasn't saying anything I didn't know. And the part of me that had puffed out my chest to encroach on Amanda's space instead of stepping back like a gentleman when she moved past me to get a drink of water grinned a little evilly.

I wasn't that guy—the type to provoke. But darn it if that wasn't exactly what Amanda had done simply by showing back up in my life. Prodded me like I was a sleeping bear and she was the stick. She had me all kinds of upside down and inside out. I simultaneously wanted to rave at her for her high-handedness and pull her close to protect her and offer her my strength.

She'd made sure I promised to create my first post tonight, even going so far as to warn that she'd turned on notifications to my posts so she could see everything and monitor on her end.

Cutest non-threatening stalker I'd ever had.

I studied Trey. "Someone ever ask you to keep a secret before?"

He snorted. "Bruh."

Right. Dumb question. Half the kid's life was probably a secret.

"But what if you thought the person was making a mistake? That she'd be better off if she told people."

He rolled up his burger wrapper and grabbed his second double-double.

Guess my question didn't deserve a response. I stared out the windshield. "I told her I'd keep her secret on one condition."

Trey's hand stopped, a grin stretching across his face. "You dog." He brought his fist up for me to bump.

I slapped his hand away. "Get your head out of the gutter. I'm going to tell John to scrub your brain with soap."

He tore into his second burger. "If not that, then what?"

Million-dollar question. Not that I'd waste that much money. "I'm not sure." I really shouldn't ask, especially given his last comment, but… "What would your condition be? And please keep your answer rated PG."

He thought a moment. "Is she pretty?"

I growled. "I told you, that's not on the table."

He rolled his eyes. "I just meant it might be nice to hang with a pretty girl. No favors. Just hanging, you know? Maybe pretend to be my girlfriend."

That's what I got for asking a teenage boy. Innuendos and the plot for a fake relationship. These kids always kept me humble, but implying the only date I could get was a fake one was a hit to my ego. Did he not even consider the fame seekers and gold diggers? If I wanted female companionship, I wouldn't have to get a girl to pretend to be with me.

The door to the coffee shop opened, and Miguel stepped out. He looked right at us like he knew we'd been there the whole time, then walked over, his tablet tucked under his arm. He opened the back door to the king cab and climbed in without a word. I handed him the other two double patty-double cheese burgers in the paper bag.

"All good?" I asked him.

"Yep."

If only I had such a ready answer to my own questions.

@Kendra11

Anyone know what Art Rooney did in his life that the NFL decided to name the sportsmanship award after him?

5

AMANDA

"*Y*ou have *got* to be kidding me." I swiped my thumb up on my cell's screen, scrolling down on the social media site, then swiped down, bringing my feed back up.

Nope. Nothing had changed. I was still staring at a picture of a white to-go bag with red palm trees along the bottom. That was it. No caption. No rhyme. No reason. No *anything*. Just a picture of a bag.

Had Peter taken too many hits to the head? Maybe the lasting effects of a bad helmet-to-helmet play? Or maybe he was just messing with me?

I knew he didn't do social media, but I hadn't thought I'd need to spell out every step for him.

Step one: Take a photo of something *interesting*.

Step two: Write a small caption with at least a few words as to why you're posting the pic.

Masterclass would include hashtags, engaging your

followers by posing a question, and possibly tagging of other people. At that speed, we'd never work our way up to story features, emojis, or GIFs. And how sad would a GIFless world be? But social media wasn't rocket science, and I knew for a fact football players had to remember more complex plays than point, click, post, and caption.

With my thumb and pointer finger, I enlarged the picture. Maybe I'd missed some important detail hidden somewhere?

"What are you looking at so intently?" Molly asked.

Betsy snatched the phone out of my hands.

"Hey!"

"What? What's going on?" Jocelyn's voice came through the laptop's speakers. The computer had been set on a bar stool and angled so Jocelyn could see the rest of us sewing girls through the camera. She'd moved three hours north to be closer to her boyfriend, both of them tired of the long-distance thing, which meant we got the AI version of Jocelyn at our weekly sewing sessions.

I used the term "sewing" loosely. Only three-fifths of us actually sewed (no, not me), but without Jocelyn, the numbers were down to half. Sewing was just the guise to meet every week and hang out.

I held out my hand. "Can I have my phone back please?"

"Why'd you take Amanda's phone?" Jocelyn asked,

getting closer to the camera as if she could jump through to physically be here with us.

Nicole glanced up at me.

"I'd like to know the answer to that myself," I grumbled, even though I knew my friends would ignore me.

"She was looking at it weird," Molly said by way of explanation.

"Weird how?" Look at Jocelyn, connecting with her inner interrogator.

Betsy smirked. "Like Nicole used to look at Drew."

"Hey!" Now it was Nicole's turn to protest.

Betsy gave her a look that challenged her to try and deny the accusation.

Nicole hugged a throw pillow beside her, a sappy grin taking over her face—her leading expression when thinking about Drew now, as opposed to a few months ago when she'd loved to hate him.

"Oooohh." Jocelyn's tone changed to that one all females seemed to adopt when the topic was about to shift to someone's love life. "Hold up the phone to the screen. I want to see it too."

I settled back against the couch cushion. With Jocelyn moving out to the Double B Ranch to be with Malachi, and Molly moving in with Ben after they got married, the sewing circle location had had to move as well. (We'd previously met in Molly and Jocelyn's shared house.) Nicole had offered her home, saying it would be easier for her since she wouldn't have to find a babysitter for her eight-year-old daughter, Sierra. She had a lovely home and comfy furniture, but being there was just one more reminder that everything was changing.

"In-N-Out? Why are you love-hating on In-N-Out, Amanda?" Jocelyn sounded confused.

"I could think of some reasons," Nicole muttered.

As a vegan, I bet she could.

"Who is Peter Reynolds?" Betsy asked, looking up from the phone.

"Your old boyfriend?" Molly asked at the same time Nicole said, "The football player?"

Betsy handed my phone back, her body language practically crooning satisfaction in a *my work here is done* sort of way.

Jocelyn put her palms to her cheeks. "I don't know which one of those to address first. Amanda, you dated a pro football player?"

"We've all heard how she objectifies athletes." Betsy studied her nails as if unimpressed by Jocelyn's ability to keep up with the conversation from long distance. "The surprise would be if we discovered she'd never dated one."

Okay, yes, I had made some comments that would make certain people blush, but I had my reasons. Or *reason*, rather.

Nicole shook her head. "Amanda is all talk. In all the years we've known her, she's never seriously dated anyone. Which makes finding out she has a history with Peter Reynolds a surprise."

"How do you know who Peter Reynolds is?" I should've used one of my stealth measures of distraction and deflection, but my mouth spoke before conferring with my brain.

Nicole picked up a pair of scissors and snipped the thread off whatever it was she was working on. All this time of watching Jocelyn, Nicole, and Molly sew, and the process still looked like a pile of material to me.

"Sierra." One shoulder rose while the other fell, communicating Nicole's mixed feelings. "My daughter's love of the game is only growing."

"The game or Drew?" The peewee quarterback had extra reason to become attached to the game, as her coach could possibly end up being her new stepdad.

Nicole smiled. "Probably both."

"I feel like we've gone off topic here." Jocelyn leaned in some more.

I sighed. There was literally zero possibility of leaving without everyone knowing my past and present in regards to Peter.

"Peter and I dated in college. He's currently a player of discussion, so I've been tasked with helping him establish more of an online presence."

"Since when are fast-food bags an online presence?" Molly looked confused.

Betsy snorted. "Since jocks are obviously dumb and have opposable thumbs."

"Who broke up with whom?" Jocelyn asked.

"I thought you quit your job as a financial analyst to

pursue your passion for design, not to live out some closet desire to reenact Law and Order." Sheesh.

Jocelyn leaned back slightly. "Just trying to determine if I need to wrangle a posse or not."

"Posse? Seriously?" One of Betsy's eyebrows quirked. So much incredulity in such a small movement.

Molly's eyes shone. "Watch out. Jocelyn's gonna cowgirl up on his heinie."

I threw out my hands. "No one is going to go anywhere on anyone's backside. I broke up with him."

Nicole seemed to consider that. "You know, that could actually be worse. What did he do to make you dump him?"

Delores thought it would be a grand idea to start practicing a snare drum in my brain at that exact moment. "He didn't do anything. We didn't work out is all."

"If his idea of an engaging post is a picture of a paper bag, then I can see why." Betsy folded her arms.

My phone vibrated a notification. I was momentarily relieved at the interruption until I saw who the email was from: Jim. Wouldn't need more than one guess as to why he'd contacted me or what mood he'd be in. Only question really was whether I still had a job or not.

I unlocked the phone and tapped to open the email.

"Uh oh. She's gone from love-hate to hate-hate." Molly sounded concerned. "Peter again?"

I shook my head. "My boss. He saw Peter's post, and let's just say he's even less impressed than Betsy. He wants to see me first thing in the morning."

Molly put her hand on my arm. "Are you okay?"

I looked up and said the same thing I always did when asked that question. "I'm fine."

One day, hopefully, that would no longer be a lie.

@AmandaMurphy

Friends make every day better. Tag your bestie and tell them why you love them.

6

PETER

I had the best job on the planet, getting to play a game I'd loved since the elementary school playground. But being a professional football player was more than showing up on the field come game day. It was six a.m. wake ups with seven a.m. lifting sessions. Eight a.m. team meetings where the head coach went over the day's expectations in practice as well as what the rest of the week should look like. Throw in a review of the last game. That sort of thing.

Nine a.m. defensive meetings. Strategies discussed. Things that had been working and improvements that needed to be made. Eleven a.m. treks to the trainers to get taped up for practice. Then a couple of hours of a walk-through instead of strenuous pads-and-helmet drills. Finally, lunch, but after we'd got our grub on, it was time for more meetings. Lots of film work and specific instructions. We also had to be available to the media every day per NFL regulations, and they had access to the locker rooms to conduct their interviews whenever they wanted.

Another defensive meeting at four p.m. to reinforce anything the coaches had noticed in the day's practice. Break for dinner and the unspoken expectation that we'd study film on our own in the evening hours.

So. Many. Meetings. We spent more time in meetings than on the field, and I'd bet my daily weigh-in fine ($550 if I'm out of range) that the average fan would never guess how much time our butts spent in seats instead of on the gridiron.

My muscles were feeling the paces I'd put them through, a warm hum under my skin reminding me of the vitality flowing through my veins. Every aspect of my life was controlled self-discipline, honing my body to perfect my craft. At the moment, I was on top of my game, but the end of my career could also only be a serious injury away. NFL didn't just stand for National Football League. It also stood for Not For Long. A pro athlete's career could last as long as the blink of an eye. I had to do everything within my power to see mine last longer than that.

"Hey, Reynolds, say hi to everyone watching my vlog."

I turned toward Andrew Phipps, a rookie who'd been drafted during the second round. He held a cell phone up between us.

"Um, hi." I gave a sort of half wave and turned back toward my locker.

Andrew laughed and rotated his phone so he peered into the camera. "A man of few words, our Pete Reynolds, but man can he shed those blockers, am I right?" He moved on, presumably to get more footage for his vlog, whatever that was.

I stuffed my sweaty gym shirt and shorts from my morning lifting session into my duffle, then zipped the top closed. There were industrial washing machines that took care of game-day jerseys, but daily practice and workout laundry was each man's responsibility.

A quiet hush suppressed the laughter that normally echoed off the dark wood cubbies of each player's locker space. Mood shifts happened a lot within these walls, but the subdued "best behavior" mask could only mean one thing: media.

I slung my duffle over my shoulder and turned, hoping whatever interview the journalist wanted didn't involve me.

My gaze slammed into blue eyes frozen over by agitation. Amanda's arms were crossed in front of her chest, her mouth pinched at the corners. Background noises continued to play, but Saunderson and Avery, the guys with lockers neighboring mine, stilled.

Super. A captive audience.

"Amanda. What are you doing here?" I moved slightly to the side, trying to shield her from the other guys. Saunderson didn't even have a shirt on for goodness' sake, and he wasn't making any grabs for one either, even though a lady had entered the room.

"That was the best you could come up with? Seriously?" Steam no longer only came from the showers.

Avery oohed and flicked his fingers in a shaking motion. "Someone's in trouble."

I ignored his taunt and stepped closer to Amanda, taking her upper arm so I could direct her out of the locker room to somewhere more private.

She stiffened under my hand. Was that pain that flashed in her eyes?

Amanda looked past me. "Planning to do laundry later? You've got a perfect washboard stomach for it, Saunderson. Let me know if you need help with your whites."

My hand fell to my side. What in the name of Walter Camp had just happened? Where was Amanda, and who was this mouthy vixen in her place? The girl I'd dated had blushed like a garden of roses when she overheard how some of the guys on my college team talked about women, and now she'd taken up some *what's good for the goose is good for the gander* type of stance?

I narrowed my eyes at her, planting my hands on my hips and creating Vs with my elbows, blocking Saunderson from getting any ideas.

"No?" Amanda asked after a beat. She shrugged. "Too bad. Maybe another time." Then she returned her steely gaze to me. "We need to talk."

Anything to get her out of the locker room and away from Saunderson before he took her up on her offer. Because, yeah, there was no way *that* was happening.

"Have you eaten?" I still needed another thousand calories to reach my daily intake. Had to fuel the machine.

She made an unidentifiable noise—something between a groan, a growl, and a sigh—then shook her head.

"Smoothie bar?" The stadium had a really good one with fresh fruits and top-of-the-line protein powders to mix in. Add a spinach-apple-walnut salad and I'd be good to go.

"Fine." She turned on her heel and stomped away. After issuing Saunderson a silent warning, I followed in her wake.

She ordered a citrus trio while I opted for a berry medley. The blenders hummed to life as we found a table not far away.

I ripped open the plastic covering the disposable fork and stabbed at the bed of spinach in my salad. "Why do I get the feeling you're mad at me for some reason?"

"Oh good. You're not a complete idiot."

I stopped chewing and looked up at her.

She threw her hands wide. "A paper bag, Peter? That was the best you could come up with?"

"Oh. That."

"Yes. That. Do you know the butt-chewing I had to endure this morning? It wasn't even a foodie-type picture, which would have been bad enough. Does In-N-Out sponsor you or something? Please, help this make sense to me."

I couldn't say the burgers were bribes for information to make sure a teen stayed safe, so I didn't say anything at all.

She sat back. "I see." Her fingers massaged her forehead. "Not that Jim's going to let you post anything without pre-approval now, but in the future, if you want to do a food post, put a spin on it."

"How do you spin food?"

Her cheeks caved in as she sucked on her straw. "You know. Include a sample of your diet plan. Like, Tom Brady is gluten-free, dairy-free, and eats only organic and seasonal food. Or like J.J. Watt eats two of every meal—two breakfasts, two lunches, two dinners. I mean, the guy consumes nine thousand calories a day. Eating is his second full-time job. Then challenge your followers to see if they can eat like you for a day or even a week."

I looked at the green salad in front of me. "People do that sort of thing?" Why? Didn't they have their own lives to live?

Amanda almost smiled for the first time all evening. "Yes, and to answer your other question, they do it for fun."

My brow pulled low. "If you say so." Unless someone planned to expend the amount of energy J.J. did, consuming six chicken breasts in a single evening seemed like a good way to give yourself a stomach ache. Then something she'd said earlier finally registered. "What do you mean Jim's not going to let me post without pre-approval?"

Her mouth curved into a smile. "We're back to that *what do you mean* thing again, huh? Basically, you've earned yourself a babysitter." She spread her hands.

My gaze roamed from the top of her head to the tips of her sneakers. I hadn't had a babysitter since, uh, ever, and I wasn't quite sure what to think about having one now. I suspected that island she'd sequestered herself on had a rim of Saguaro cacti along the border, and I wasn't particularly keen on coming away looking like I'd lost a battle with a porcupine.

"I can see you're as excited about this idea as I am. Traveling all over the country with the team isn't high on my bucket list. Delores has an aversion to planes."

I took another bite, trying to act like her talking about her illness wasn't a big deal. "Do you get flare-ups after?"

She blinked at me. "Um, yeah."

They were really going to make her do something that could make her sick, all because of a social media post? Then again, they didn't know she was sick. And I'd promised not to tell anyone. Ugh.

"Why don't you just post for me? Save everyone the trouble."

She shook her head even before I'd finished talking. "This isn't a short-term thing. You and social media better learn to get along, because you're stuck with each other for as long as you put on the jersey." She took a drink. "The posts have to come from you. I'm only along as your personal tutor."

I sighed. "Fine. But that still doesn't mean you have to travel with us. You can tell me what to post—" She shook her head, so I amended, "Or I can call you before I throw anything up online and make sure it passes muster."

Her smile was sad. "That's logical, but I'm afraid Jim is past reason. He wants me there, so there I will be."

She didn't have to be. She *shouldn't* be. "Tell him. If you tell him what traveling will do to you, I'm sure he'll see that something else can be worked out."

Her grip tightened around her disposable cup. "You promised you wouldn't."

"On one condition."

"Which I'm still waiting for."

Yeah, so was I. "Amanda." I could intimidate men three times her size, surely I could—

"Peter," she mimicked in the same tone.

My lungs deflated. Guess I had myself a babysitter.

. . .

@CondorsOfficial

Watch this #replay of Peter Reynolds sacking Russel Wilson, then in what's becoming his signature move, offering a hand to help the QB up. #highlights

7

AMANDA

"So, I thought I'd give you a quick rundown of how social media works and what sort of things Jim expects to see on your feed." I pulled the small notebook and pen from my bag, which I'd put there earlier for this purpose. Normally, I'd jot everything down in Notes and then attach the digital file to a text or email. With Peter's aversion to online community, however, I thought it'd be safer if he had a physical copy of dos and don'ts he could reference.

Instead of showing an interest in anything in front of me, Peter looked around at the deserted stadium. The employee behind the smoothie counter cleaned up the machines. A light flicked off farther down the open space.

"They're starting to close, so we'll have to take this elsewhere."

I clicked my pen shut. "Right. How about the coffee shop two blocks over?"

Peter rubbed at his shoulder. "It's kind of been a long day, and I was looking forward to sitting back and relaxing on the couch. We can always go to my place. Or yours, if you'd prefer."

Go to Peter's? That would be about as smart as tossing a lit cigarette out the window during the dry months of late summer. Both had the potential for disaster, and both put me in danger of getting burned.

As loath as I was to admit it, five years had done nothing to cool my feelings for Peter. I still found him too attractive for his own good, what with his hypnotically changing eyes, the strong cut of his jaw, and the intelligent tilt to his brow. Not to mention his sheer size. Something that probably frightened or overwhelmed other women oddly comforted me. As if there were a correlation between his build and ability to protect me, to fight unseen foes.

Utterly ridiculous, but there it was. Five years later and I was still in love with my first, last, and only boyfriend. And still not in a position to do anything about it. His body was the tool of his trade—a trade he executed with finesse—while mine operated with all the grace of a newborn giraffe suffering vertigo. I'd only hold Peter back. I couldn't do it to him five years ago, and I couldn't do it to him now.

Oh, but how nice it would be if I could.

"Amanda?" His deep voice brought me out of my

introspection and saved me the bittersweet aftertaste of remembering what being with Peter had been like.

Wonderful. It—*he*—had been wonderful.

"Your place or mine?"

Neither, please. But that didn't seem to be on the table. Guess I'd have to go for home-field advantage and spend the drive across town reminding myself why Peter was forbidden fruit.

"Mine. You can follow me over."

He nodded and gathered his trash, dumping his smoothie cup and salad bowl in the receptacle.

I fished my keys out of my purse and picked up my cup. I'd only managed to drink about half. If I tried to chug the rest, I'd end up with a brain freeze. Better to nurse the drink on the drive home.

Peter said he'd meet me at the south entrance once he got his truck from the player's parking area. I didn't have to wait long until his silver F-150 pulled up behind me. He flashed his lights to let me know it was him. As if I could forget the vehicle in which we'd spent so many nights cuddled in the bed, staring up at the star-studded sky.

My throat dried at the memory and the fact Peter would soon be making himself comfortable in my space. My hand shot toward the leftover smoothie in the cup holder, gripping the lid to lift the drink from its spot. The seal broke, and I watched in horror, one hand on the steering wheel and the other holding a now-unattached lid, as gravity pulled the pink paper to-go cup toward my lap.

Cold liquid seeped into my shirt and pants. I sucked in a breath, biting my tongue against a choice word that tried to form.

Fantastic. Now I was as much of a mess on the outside as I was on the inside.

By the time I made it home, my skin had started to itch. I wanted nothing more than to strip myself of the sodden mess. Okay, not exactly true. I wanted more than that, but I'd settle for some clean clothes.

"What happened to you?" Peter asked as he stepped out of his truck.

"I was born," I muttered under my breath, because really, sometimes the better question seemed to be what *hadn't* happened to me.

I slid my key into the lock of the apartment building's glass front door and turned until the mechanism inside clicked. Peter followed me down the hall like a looming shadow.

When I first moved to the city, it took me a little while to find an apartment on the ground level. There were plenty of places available, but those in my budget were in buildings without elevators and with vacancies on floors other than the first. On good days, I could make it up a flight of stairs, but most days weren't good, and even when they were, my body would give out trying to climb three or four flights. Seriously. Might as well have been Everest. So when I stumbled upon this little place being advertised online, I forked over the exorbitant security deposit and moved in.

Now, as I opened the front door and Peter stepped into my apartment, I recognized my mistake. Peter probably lived in a mansion in the hills with enough space that we could each coexist and maintain our personal bubbles.

My place…well, Peter sort of absorbed it. Two steps in and my apartment felt like it had shrunk in front of my eyes. Had the walls only ever been that far apart? How had the room seemed bigger this morning?

"Cute place," Peter said behind me. "It feels…" He looked around.

I followed his line of sight, trying to see things from his perspective. My brown leather sofa was worn three shades lighter in the middle of the cushions from all the years of use it had seen. A large print of the Anza-Borrego Desert in spring with an array of purple and yellow flowers in the foreground hung over the couch. My coffee table had been a local find, made of hairpin legs and a reclaimed-wood top. Underneath the furniture lay a large rug of creams, soft greys, and butter yellows.

"Homey."

I set my keys and purse on the counter, a little unnerved at his pronouncement. "It *is* my home. How else should it feel?"

Great. Now I was channeling Betsy. She possessed a snark I couldn't—and didn't want—to pull off.

I grabbed the hem of my shirt and tugged down, peeling the fabric away from my skin. "I'm going to go change."

Peter lowered his hulking frame onto the plush leather of my sofa.

Darn it. My place looked even more homey with Peter in it.

I retreated into my room and slammed the door a little harder than necessary. Toeing off my shoes, I unhooked my pants button, then tugged off my jeans. I stretched out the neck hole of my shirt and lifted it up by the shoulders so I wouldn't smear citrus smoothie all over my face.

My lips pushed to the side. Should I go ahead and change my sports bra too? I'd sweated during my afternoon fever, so might as well put on all new fresh clothes while I was already changing.

I crossed my arms and tried to wiggle my fingers under the band of my racerback sports bra. *What in the world?* The thing felt like someone had used liquid nails to adhere it to my skin. I leaned over. Bent back. Stretched to the side. Really, I might as well have been doing body rolls, but then—*yes!*—I finally managed to slip the tips of my fingers between my ribs and the elastic band. Ah-ha! Didn't need to find a crowbar after all.

Shimmying my fingers higher, I lifted my elbows and took a few quick breaths like weight lifters do before getting into position in a heat. Some got a workout from hundred-pound weights, others knew one could be had by wrestling a small undergarment off one's body.

Using the wall as an anchor to stretch and contort myself at just the right angle, I shook my butt and shimmied my whole body, inching the elastic up my arms and around my shoulders—because, yes, removing a sports bra really was a whole-body experience. Halfway up, with my arms a pretzel in front of my face, my muscles quivered and my grip started to slip.

No, no, no!

I reached for the slipping material, bending my knees to help my reach, and slammed my thigh into my dresser.

"Ouch!" That would leave a bruise.

"Amanda? You okay? Do you need help?"

I froze, deer-in-the-headlights style, and stared at the door. Or rather, in the direction of the door. All I could see was a swatch of stretchy underwear in front of my face.

"Don't come in!" Janet Jackson's wardrobe malfunction during the Halftime Show would pale in comparison if Peter somehow opened the door and saw me in my current condition.

With renewed frenzy, I pliéd with the speed of a ballerina after half a dozen energy drinks while frantically trying to get ahold of even an inch of fabric. My fingers brushed something other than my own skin. Yes! I jumped and shimmied and turned, spazzing every which way to get purchase. And slammed my hip, this time into the corner of the dresser.

"Amanda, tell me you're okay or I swear I'll break this door down."

"Don't even think about it, Peter!" I shrieked. My shoulders cramped and my arms were starting to tingle. If I had a pair of scissors, I'd cut myself out of this torture device, but one thing was certain: I had to unstick myself before Peter played the hero and saw more of me than anyone had the right to.

In one last valiant attempt, I pulled my shoulders in and stretched as far as my arms would go. *There! Got it!* Channeling my inner Hulk, I ripped that thing clear off my head and flung it across the room.

Panting, I covered myself in case the door flew open. "I'll be out in a minute!"

"Sixty seconds or I'm coming in." His tone said he wasn't kidding.

I threw on clothes as quickly as possible, ignoring my mental image of Delores (I pictured her as a stern-faced schoolmarm with a mean streak—the kind that got pleasure from rapping students' knuckles with yard sticks) holding a clipboard in her hand and making notes of all the places she planned to poke with a branding iron later.

Fifty-eight-point-three seconds later, I swung open my bedroom door, flushed, out of breath, and feeling like I'd just wrestled a slippery boa constrictor and had barely come out the victor.

Not far from the truth.

"What was all the banging? I was worried you were fighting off an intruder or something." Peter's sharp gaze looked past me as if searching for said intruder. His large muscles bulged beneath his clothes, and he looked like a tiger ready to pounce.

"Nothing like that." I breezed past him, hoping my blithe tone and unworried air would turn off the suspicious glint in his eyes. "Should we get started?" I folded my legs under me on the sofa and retrieved the pen and notepad.

Peter hovered over me. Towered, really.

It took a considerable amount of effort on my part not to squirm. I didn't look up, but I could feel his gaze like a laser on the top of my head.

I cleared my throat and ran my tongue over the roof of my mouth, trying to moisten what had suddenly gone parched.

"Right. So, basics."

"I know the basics." Peter dropped down onto the couch beside me.

Physics in action: when a two-hundred-sixty-pound mass exerts a sudden downward force on a shared sofa cushion, one hundred thirty previously-stationary pounds will experience a sudden increase in velocity.

In short, my sofa became a bounce house.

I yipped as my butt sailed off the cushion. I hovered in the air, then landed, tumbling toward Peter thanks to the sinkhole his weight created beside me.

"Whoa there." He pulled me to his side.

No, that wasn't right. I was already plastered to him like a second skin. His arm supported me as I peeled myself away, his muscles flexing under my palm. My cheeks flamed as I pushed away. As soon as I let go and Peter dropped his hand, I found myself rolling back toward him like a ball on unlevel ground. I leaned to the opposite side, determined not to be sucked into Peter's vortex.

In more ways than one.

I thought heavy thoughts and said, "How about a thirty-day challenge?"

He stretched his arm along the back of the couch, his thumb brushing against my shoulder.

Nerves at that point flared to life, demanding all my attention.

What had I been saying? Something about...

I bolted up and fairly leaped across the living room. "Water?"

"Sure." Peter's eyes glowed green.

The little turd! He'd known exactly what he was doing.

I stomped the short distance to the kitchen and yanked open the refrigerator. Grabbing a bottle of water, I was tempted to unscrew the lid and dump it over his head. Instead, I chucked it at his face.

Plastic crinkled as he caught the cold bottle before it made contact with his nose. Too bad his job description included snatching flying objects out of the air.

He chuckled before chugging half the bottle. "You said something about a challenge."

I leaned against the counter. The more space between Peter and me, the better. "A daily post challenge. We'll write them all out now so you won't have to come up with content every day. The first day could be to post a pic from wherever you are and invite people to comment with pics of where they are."

"Sounds like an invitation for trouble if you ask me."

Hmmm...maybe letting everyone know his location wouldn't be the best idea, with how crazy some fans (and haters) could be.

"What about introducing a teammate? Maybe a rookie who the fans may not know much about yet."

He seemed to consider. "That could work."

"Good. I'll write that down for a day."

We bandied about other ideas, settling on participating in certain hashtags like #momandpopbusinessowners to support small, local businesses and #22pushupchallenge to raise awareness for the estimated twenty-two veterans who committed suicide every day, as well as some classic posts like 'this or that', #TBT (Throwback Thursday), and #TuesdayTip.

I chewed on the tip of the pen. "These are good."

"I sense a *but* coming."

How to word this in a way that wouldn't make him bristle? "It's just, you have a unique opportunity here. A platform and reach because of your name and position that others would love to have. Imagine how many people you could inspire beyond football if you shared your story."

He stared at me the way I imagined he looked at offensive linemen across the line of scrimmage. Then he blinked, pulled his phone out, and started scrolling.

"What are you doing?"

"Looking through your posts to see what this *inspiration* looks like." His thumb flicked up his screen. "Seems to me you're in a unique situation to be an inspiration to other people struggling with health issues and yet"—he turned his phone around, a picture of me smiling broadly like I lived in an untouched world—"and yet posts like this are all I see."

I knew what he was getting at, but... "It's not the same."

"You're asking me to be vulnerable and share something painful with people who may not understand. Sounds exactly the same to me." He leaned forward and rested his forearms on his knees. "You want a challenge? How about this. I'll share my story with the world if you share yours."

@AmandaMurphy

Am I the only person on the planet who has never seen #LOTR?

@Tolking

@AmandaMurphy YES! You need a movie marathon ASAP

PETER

he sun glinted off the metal of the Boeing airplane fueling up to take the Condors to Salt Lake City. Not every team had a private plane like the Patriots. The rest of us plebians traveled by aircraft chartered from major airlines. There were perks to not flying commercial, but I'd often wondered what kind of frequent flyer miles I could rack up from away games August through January (depending on how well the team did in the playoffs).

"Anyone check the weather report for Sunday?" Phipps asked with a grimace. "They're predicting three to five inches of snow with a wind chill putting temps into the single digits."

Condor's quarterback, Grant Hawthorne, grinned. "Balmy."

Phipps shivered as if the frigid mountain winds had

already settled into his bones. "Says the Minnesotan. I'm from South Texas. Anything below seventy-five is freezing."

I elbowed the rookie. "At least we aren't headed to Green Bay. They've had how many Snow Bowls now?"

"Let's see." Hawthorne seemed to consider. "1977 against the Vikings. Although the Bucs in '85 would've been even more unprepared, coming from Tampa Bay and all. The scoreboard showed it too."

"The Seahawks had a hard time in 2007 as well," I added.

Phipps groaned, then turned toward the east, arms outstretched.

"What are you doing?" Grant laughed.

"Make fun of me all you want. I'm soaking up as much of the sun as I can."

A feminine form stepped out from behind a wall of suit jackets. While the majority of our entourage was of the male variety, there were a few women who traveled with the team—a couple of trainers and a member of the special teams coaching staff. However, the petite frame dwarfed by my larger-than-average teammates belonged to none of those ladies.

I knew, because they didn't have the power to make my heart race like a hormonal teenager spying his crush across the room. Even with Amanda's *Keep Away* sign stamped on her forehead and the actual words she'd said to me to put distance between us, my heart still yearned for her. Even after all this time. After everything that had happened.

The way I saw it, I had two choices. I could learn from the past and guard my heart against Amanda's special charms, or...

I sighed. Who was I kidding? There wasn't really a choice at all. I couldn't leave her on the isolated island she'd built for herself. To fight an unseen battle all alone. For whatever reason, she'd convinced herself she didn't need anyone.

It still hurt, being cut out of her life. But this couldn't be about me. Well, it couldn't be *all* about me, at least. If, while learning to trust others again, Amanda opened her eyes enough to see what I wanted—what I had *always* wanted: a partner in life, for better or worse, in health *and* sickness—well, then, all the better.

"Amanda." I called her over.

She smiled and walked around Jeb Abeson, the team's kicker. She had a lightweight jacket draped over her arm.

"Ready for the flight? Shouldn't be too long from here to Salt Lake. Only about three hours or so. Do you think because it's a shorter flight that there won't be as severe—"

Amanda's eyes flashed, and she turned to put her hand on Grant's arm. "Are you sure they have you playing the right position?" She smiled up at him sweetly.

My head snapped back. What had just happened?

Grant's eyebrows jumped. "Excuse me?"

Phipps turned from his reptile impersonation, shock unhinging his jaw. "Grant Hawthorne is one of the greatest quarterbacks of all time. He's going to be in the Hall of Fame one day. Have you seen his stats?"

Amanda smirked. "I'm not saying he isn't a really good quarterback. But I do think he's got an even better tight end." She looked meaningfully at Grant's backside.

Heat flushed my face. Anger? Embarrassment? Yeah, definitely both of those.

I loosely gripped Amanda's upper arm and propelled her past my stunned teammates. "Excuse us, guys."

Only when we were far enough away to not be overheard did I release my hold on her arm. "Do you mind explaining what that was?"

She stared over my left shoulder. "I don't know what you're talking about."

"No?" My nostrils flared.

Five years was a long time, and people changed, but did they really change *that* much? This was the second time Amanda had shocked me with a borderline crass statement. If a guy had made a comment like that about a woman, he'd be considered a chauvinistic pig (and rightly so).

But Amanda? I'd never imagined such a thing coming out of her mouth. First, the inappropriate comment about Saunderson's abs, now Hawthorne's "tight end."

My jaw flexed as my gaze narrowed. Amanda wouldn't look at me. She rubbed at her fingers, something I'd noticed her doing a number of times before. In fact, when she'd said she could do laundry on the tight end's—the correct use of the phrase—washboard abs, her mouth had been pinched in pain. And just now—

It all added up to a sad sum.

"You'd really rather people think you've picked up the language and practices of a locker room than learn the truth?"

Her gaze flicked to mine before darting away again. "Maybe I just don't want to live a double-standard life. Guys—"

"That's not going to fly with me. Maybe you've tricked other people into thinking whatever it is you're more comfortable with them thinking—although for the life of me I don't know why—but you forget that I know you, Amanda. I know the girl from small-town middle America who used to blush and avert her eyes if there was ever a shirts vs. skins pickup game. You forget that I've memorized your every feature. That I'm familiar with all your expressions."

Her shoulders collapsed an inch, and the defiant set to her chin softened. Then her cheek twitched as she tried to stifle a grin. "I'm sure women say all sorts of outlandish things to those guys. Grant probably won't even remember my comment in an hour."

A growl built in my throat. "And yet it's something I'll never manage to forget."

"Looks like it's time to board." Amanda breezed past me, effectively shutting the door on the conversation.

But we weren't done. Not by a long shot.

I followed Amanda down the gangplank, stopping and shuffling forward as we bottle-necked through the plane's door and down the narrow aisle. She side-stepped into a row of seats, taking the one by the window. When I sat beside her, she lifted her head in surprise.

That's right. I'm not going to be so easy to get rid of this time around.

I smiled at her and shoved earbuds into my ears. Some of the guys liked to strategize for the upcoming game on the flight over, but I always listened to my pre-game playlist.

Everyone finished boarding, and the plane taxied to the runway. Amanda slipped on her jacket.

I pulled the small speaker out of one ear, lowering the volume of "Eye of the Tiger." "Cold?"

"Not yet, but I don't want to get cold either." She eyed my headphones. "What are you listening to, and have you not heard of a thing called blue tooth? Phone with a cracked screen. Same truck you drove pre-NFL contract. Headphones ten years out of date. Making poor financial decisions, Reynolds?"

I ignored her teasing and handed her one of the earbuds. Depending on who was asked, she'd either hit the nail on the head or was way off the mark. "Just getting into the right frame of mind for the game. These are my fight songs, so to speak."

Her mouth took a bemused turn as she settled the small bud into her ear. She looked at me, her eyes laughing. "Could you have picked anything more on the nose?"

"Hey! "Eye of the Tiger" is a classic. *Rocky* is one of the greatest films ever made, and if this song could help Rocky Balboa with the big fight, then I don't see how you can laugh at me for listening to it before a game."

"I'll let you keep your delusions about Rocky being such a fantastic movie, unless your argument is that it's somehow so bad that it's good."

"Bad?" I coughed. How could an iconic film about the rise of an underdog ever be bad?

"And I'll grant you that the music is catchy," she continued.

"It's more than catchy."

"But there have to be better fight songs that get you pumped up. Something with stronger lyrics or a better beat."

Was she even listening to the music streaming through the speakers? "You're crazy."

She laughed. "Probably, but not about this."

"I bet more people would agree with me on the superiority of my choice."

She leaned forward. "And I bet people could come up with *lots* more better songs."

My smile climbed up my cheeks. "More better?"

She play-slapped my arm. "Shut up. You know what I mean."

I pulled out my phone. "Should we settle this argument on social media, my posting warden?"

Amanda rolled her eyes. "Warden shmarden. But yeah. Something like a vote or argument settlement makes a good post because you're calling your audience to engage with you."

I leaned on the armrest between us while holding my phone up with my other hand. "Scootch closer."

Amanda's shoulder pressed against mine as she fit her face into the phone camera's frame. The cords of the headphones dangled between us, connecting us. She smiled for the picture and I did the same, staring at her face on the screen instead of the camera's lens. My thumb tapped the shutter button.

Amanda moved away from me. I had to remind myself that the game had four quarters. I'd barely started playing, and for something more important than the Vince Lombardi trophy: Amanda Murphy's heart.

I typed up a quick post to accompany our picture.

@PeterReynolds

Help settle an argument. Is "Eye of the Tiger" the greatest of all times or can you think of a better fight song?

. . .

I tilted the screen toward Amanda. "How's this?"

She read the short caption over. "Good. You asked a question to engage your audience, but how about we add a few hashtags to the equation as well." She held out her palm for my phone and I passed it.

A few taps to the delete button and her thumbs flew over the screen. She handed it back.

@PeterReynolds

Help settle an argument. Is "Eye of the Tiger" the #GOAT or can you think of a better #FightSong? #WhoIsRight #WhatsOnYourPlaylist

She looked at me and smiled. "You don't even really need me."

That's where she was wrong. She may have thought she didn't need me, but I *knew* I needed her.

@Reese98

@PeterReynolds For sure it's Eye of the Tiger! Love that song!

@JMo

@PeterReynolds I really like to listen to Here Comes the Boom by Nelly when I need to get pumped up.

@HeidiSimms

@JM I can't hear of that song without thinking of Kevin James. LOL. What a great movie.

2.3k Likes 621 comments 211 shares

I'd call myself the walking dead, but I couldn't even accomplish that simple function. Walking: so easy a toddler could do it. Yet there I lay, cheek pressed against a pillow, all my energy being used to lift my hand and press a button on the remote to change the channel on the TV.

When people made an offhand remark about going home to crash, they usually meant they planned to chill with Netflix and put their feet up.

If only crashing had such an innocuous meaning to me. More like Delores drink-driving through my immune system, leaving havoc in her wake—which left me stripped of any energy for at least a day or more.

But at least I wasn't in bed. Custer may have made his last stand at the Battle of Little Bighorn, but my last stand occurred at the Battle of Sheets and Mattress.

Maybe it was silly, but making it to the sofa was a small victory for me. For some reason, staying in bed when I crashed was almost like conceding a win to Delores. Making my feet carry me the short distance to the couch was my small act of rebellion.

Thankfully, the hotel the franchise had put us up in had couches in a small sitting area in their rooms. Otherwise my white hotel sheets would have also served as white flags of surrender. On days when I felt like death warmed over, I had to find my victories where I could, however small they may seem.

The announcers' voices projected from the TV speakers as the camera panned out over the field and the audience in the stadium. Even with the low temperatures, Mustang fans had turned out in their orange and blue to show their support for their team. Breaths puffed visibly in front of faces red from the cold. When the camera stopped on a couple with a blanket the Condors' shade of burgundy, the pair jumped up and turned around, holding the blanket out. Vulture wings, those of a California Condor specifically, spread out on both sides from the middle.

I smiled. Peter and his teammates wouldn't be without a cheering section. My smile waned as I remembered I was supposed to be there too, yelling until my voice went hoarse. Right then, however, I was more apt to believe I'd never move again. The post office would have to be notified of a change of address: 123 Blue Sofa, Posh Hotel, CO.

My phone buzzed by my head. I'd turned off the ringer earlier because of a headache. Betsy's name lit up on the screen. My finger hovered over the green *accept* circle.

Out of all my friends, Betsy was the most intuitive. Honestly, I was kind of surprised I'd been able to keep Delores a secret from her all this time. By now, she probably wondered how I hadn't gotten sued for sexual harassment, since I'd had to say so many shocking things in front of her to keep her off the scent of the truth.

If I answered, I wouldn't be able to fake that everything was fine. She'd see past my smokescreen and demand to know what was wrong. And then I'd be where I was with past friends, where I was with my family: simply a person making more out of something than was necessary with a sickness that was all in my head.

I couldn't go through that again.

Pushing aside the guilt, I moved my thumb over to the red *decline* stamp and pressed. Later, I'd call her back. When I could infuse liveliness into my voice once more.

The Mustangs had first possession of the ball, and Trevor Bryce started the game by making a deep left-side kick. The Mustangs' special teams' player didn't signal for a fair catch, instead tucking the ball safely in his arm and running down field. He didn't get far before being tackled by our guys in burgundy and navy.

I turned onto my back and palmed my phone. My coworker, Janet, had agreed to snap some pictures behind the scenes and on the field so I could post to the team's social media accounts. I thumbed through and picked a profile shot of quarterback Grant Hawthorne with his hand on the shoulder pad of his favorite wide receiver, Calvin Moore. While Hawthorne threw to other players, he seemed to have a rhythm with Moore that opposing teams had a hard time stopping. Which was pretty much the caption I added to the photo before posting.

I switched to my personal account and tapped the notifications icon. Peter had tagged me in his fight song post, which seemed to be getting a good response with his followers. Of course, not all comments were about the greatness or lameness of "Eye of the Tiger." Some speculated about who I was to Peter.

No one. Not anymore.

I waited for the justification of my decision to end things with him to wash over me like peroxide on an open wound. A sting at first, yes, but with the knowledge that the hurt served a greater purpose.

Except the reassurance never came.

The more I stared at our picture together, the greater the sinkhole in my heart became. He knew about Delores and hadn't judged my health on what he could see with his own eyes. Hadn't jumped to conclusions based on the doctor's inability to find the cause of my internal suffering.

What would the last five years have been like with Peter by my side? But no, that was my tiredness talking (and I was *so* tired) and my selfishness. Being with me would have been the same as clipping his wings.

I turned my eyes away from my phone screen to watch the game. Players readied on the line of scrimmage, and then the ball was snapped. Like lightning, Peter shot from the line, spun around the momentum of the blocker to shed him, then dove for the back and passing arm of the Mustangs' QB. The quarterback folded himself around the football before falling like a sack of potatoes to the ground. Peter lay on top of him for a moment before pushing himself up. Instead of doing a victory dance or pumping his fists in the air like other players, Peter offered the QB his hand and helped the opposing player up, slapping him good naturedly on the back before walking to line up again.

More proof that my Condor was made to fly.

I opened Twitter to live tweet the game. Unbiased reporting on the official page, fandom taunting on my personal account.

@CondorsOfficial

Did you see that sack from @PeterReynolds? #Defense #SundayIsForFootball #CondorsSoar

. . .

The game continued, as did I, posting updates on one account and verbal smackdown and gloating on the other. The game ended 31-14, another win for the Condors. The reporters on the field smiled and stuck their microphones into panting players' faces, asking their take on the game and the team's chances at the Super Bowl.

My head felt fuzzy, the back of my eyelids having turned into sandpaper. The voices droned, getting quieter. Which was weird, since I hadn't turned the volume down.

Pounding made me blink. Funny, the light had been shining through the window a second ago. Pink hues softened the white walls now.

Bang. Bang.

I touched my temple. Either my pounding headache had turned audible or someone very insistent was at my door.

"Just a minute," I yelled. Okay, I squeaked.

More banging.

I set my feet on the floor and paused for the room to stop spinning. When the carousel halted to let me off, I stood, fingers gliding along the wall as I baby-stepped forward. You know, just in case I needed something solid to keep me from falling on my face.

The door creaked on its hinges when I pulled it open a smidge.

Peter glowered at me from the other side. I'd never

gotten it before, Mr. Darcy's appeal. How was a man always scowling at you at all attractive?

Now I knew. It wasn't so much the frown—although Peter's furrowed brow somehow caused a visceral reaction low in my gut—as the depth behind the intense look.

"Why am I always threatening to break down doors when you're around, Amanda?" He put a meaty paw on the wood grain under the metal room numbers and pushed, both the door open and his way past me.

I leaned against the door, my weight shutting it and its solidness holding me up. Symbiotic relationships were a good thing.

Peter spun, his eyes narrowing on my white-knuckled grip on the knob.

Reflexes had me opening my mouth, a shocking retort on my tongue to deflect his focus.

His jaw ticked, his eyes darkening from hunter-green to dark brown. The shade of anger. "Don't."

My cheeks heated. I'd never really gotten past the embarrassment of the things I'd said to save myself, but I'd gotten good at not letting that shame pinken my ivory skin. But with one word, one look, Peter stripped me of the comfort of my false identity. I may as well have been standing in front of him naked, I felt so exposed.

The heat rose to the tips of my ears.

He stared at me, his feet braced apart.

In the face of such restrained power and raw

emotion, any woman would have gone weak in the knees.

That's my story and I'm sticking to it.

Peter sighed and shook his head before he took two giant steps toward me. I swayed forward at the same time Peter bent then swung me up into his arms.

His chest was solid beneath my palm, his muscles corded bands of dedication to his job, to making him the best he could be.

His eyes changeling eyes stared down at me, his arms tightening at my back and under my knees. "Maybe this wasn't the best idea," he mumbled. I got the impression he was talking more to himself than to me.

But I agreed with him. If I was going to come away from this assignment with my heart in enough pieces to put back together instead of completely shattered, I needed to make sure there was distance between us.

"Put me down." Good job mouth. Very believable. My gaze snagged on my fingers clutching the fabric of Peter's shirt. I rolled my eyes.

If only every part of me were obedient.

Peter chuckled as I loosened my grip on him and smoothed out the wrinkles I'd created. Mistake. Smoothing wrinkles meant running my hand over his chest. His pulse pounded under my palm. I peeked up.

Yep. His eyes had changed yet again, darkening to a hunter green.

He cradled me to him and walked toward the

couch, laying me gently on the cushions. He knelt down in front of me, bringing himself to my eye level.

"I'm fine," I said, beating him to the punch. My eyes darted away from his knows-too-much gaze.

His large palm slid across my jaw, slight pressure urging my face and gaze back to his.

I swallowed and forced myself to look into the swirl of color in his irises. Any bravado I could cover up with, he'd strip away. I hated to appear weak and didn't want to see myself that way in the reflection of his eyes.

"My condition. I know what it is now," Peter said.

Oh goodie. Adding brain fatigue to my list of current symptoms, because I had *no* idea what Peter was talking about.

His thumb caressed my forehead, presumably to smooth out my furrowed brow. "I keep your secret on one condition?"

Oh right. *That.* "Which is?"

His gaze moved between my eyes. "Authenticity."

"Peter—"

"With me. Authenticity with me. No lying. No sugarcoating. You're upfront about how you feel and what you're thinking. No exceptions."

I could envision Molly waving truth pom-poms and cheering this deal on. My friend had a strict honesty policy—one that had gotten her fired from her job at a Montessori preschool when one of her students had gone fishing in her purse and found a feminine hygiene product and asked what it was. Yup. Molly had answered that four-year-old's question.

It wasn't that I was against the truth or lied all the time. I just had a strong self-preservation instinct, and it seemed to kick in weird (and sometimes inappropriate) ways.

"I'm serious, Amanda." Peter's Mr. Darcy impression was back.

Peter already knew about Delores. Not sugarcoating would cost me my pride, but that was a small price to pay to keep my friends and strangers alike from looking at me first with pity and then with scorn.

"Okay. I agree."

Peter's lips, which had been pressed in a firm line, relaxed to a small smile. "Good. Now, tell me how you are."

"I'm—"

"If you say fine, so help me, Amanda…"

I swallowed down the word. Right. No sugarcoating. A sense of relief flooded through my limbs, taking with it the last dregs of my energy. I sank into the cushions of the couch, lying across the length. "I've been better." I gave a humorless chuckle. "I've also been worse."

"Is there anything I can do?"

I shrugged the shoulder not pinned under me. "Not really. I just need to rest."

He seemed to consider, then nodded. He stood, and I thought he'd leave.

I thought wrong.

Instead of exiting the same way he'd entered, Peter slid his hands under my head and shoulders, lifting. He sat, then lowered my head onto his lap.

"What are you doing?" How could I keep my distance when he'd made himself my pillow?

He picked up the remote and changed the channel to watch ESPN Sports Center. "What does it look like? I'm watching TV."

I stared up at him. "Pretty sure you have a TV in your own room."

He turned up the volume. "Shh. I'm trying to listen."

Now what? I didn't have the energy to lift my head, much less push a two-hundred-and-sixty-pound professional athlete—basically a human brick wall—out the door.

Peter's hand settled on my head, his fingers playing with my hair. "Relax, Amanda. Rest."

His voice and the way his fingertips massaged my scalp bypassed conscious thought and turned my muscles to goo.

I wanted to protest, but each stroke of his hand made my eyes heavier. And his lap made the perfect pillow. My neck wasn't wrenched to an odd angle from being too high or curved from being too flat.

Peter seemed to be my Goldilocks. He fit me just right.

. . .

@AmandaMurphy

Can't wait to see my team score another victory #CondorsSoar

@PeterReynold

Thank you to all the fans who came out to support us!

PETER

I spent hours upon hours poring over game plans and observing the opposition—learning their weaknesses and vulnerabilities and then devising strategies to make those weak points my strengths so that I and my teammates could come out victors.

I'd heard advice among some of the guys that the same approach could be taken with women, especially any who may've been playing hard to get. I could see the logic, but something didn't sit right with the visualization.

While Amanda had napped in Salt Lake, her head on my lap, my fingers remembering the softness of her silky hair, I'd figured out why the advice wasn't right.

Amanda wasn't my opponent. At least, I didn't want her to be, and I didn't want her to see me that way either. Instead, I wanted us to be on the same team. Me on her team and her on mine. Working together toward the same goal. If someone or some*thing* sought to take her down, I'd be her blocker. If by chance I couldn't stop the forward play, then I'd be somewhere soft she could land.

Now the question was, how could I get her to see me and trust me as her teammate and let me in instead of shutting me out?

The lights coming from the windows of the familiar bungalow shone in the darkness of the early evening. Night came on quicker this time of year, chasing people indoors and embracing them with time with family. Whatever that looked like.

Lanky forms of teen boys moved in front of the window, their bodies in between that of boyhood and full-on adult male. They worked together to set a long table, their laughter inaudible from the distance but seen on their faces and in their body language.

I grabbed the three pies I'd picked up at the grocery store on the way over—apple, cherry, and pumpkin— and opened the truck door. With the sun's disappearance, there was a nip in the air. Nothing arctic like Salt Lake had been, but enough that I'd be reaching for a flannel if I stayed outside any length of time.

I didn't bother knocking before making my way inside. In a sense, this house still felt a bit like home. As much a home as I'd ever had growing up. And although the ragtag bunch within its walls changed throughout the years, anyone under this roof would be family.

"Peter." A deep, jovial voice rang out. John smiled at me behind his full beard from the other side of the room. "Glad you could make it," he said as he set a large pot roast encircled by potatoes and carrots down on the table.

There weren't many rules at Boys to Men. In fact, there were only three.

Respect others.

Respect yourself.

Get your butt in a seat around the table for family dinner night. No excuses.

My old room downstairs may have a different occupant now, but I still tried to abide by house rules as much as possible.

I placed the pies on an ancient sideboard with more nicks than the New York basketball team. "I brought desert."

Miguel lifted his head from typing something into his tablet. He eyed the pies. "Apple?"

I swung my arm over his thin shoulder and pulled him to my side. "I got you man."

He spared me a glance before returning his concentration to the device in his hands.

Trey and Mason exited the kitchen carrying food—dinner rolls and salad respectively. After setting the platters on the table, they pulled out chairs and sat.

"Where's Ezra?" I asked over the scraping sound the foot of the chair made against the wood floors.

The boys looked at each other across the table.

"He's visiting his mom," John answered.

Every boy who lived at Boys to Men had his own story, and none included a white picket fence.

While John had been a surrogate father to some totally without, he mostly stepped into shoes vacated because of parents' poor decisions. Some of those decisions had led to jail time, as was the case with Ezra's parents. Angry and hurt, Ezra had responded in what professionals considered "unhealthy" ways, getting himself kicked out of his foster home and sent to John.

One of my "brothers" while I lived at Boys to Men referred to John Allen as Pan because he surrounded himself with society's lost boys. But unlike the fictional character bearing my own name, John helped those in his care to grow and mature at great personal cost to himself.

"Shall we bless the food and dig in?" John folded his hands and bowed his head. "Dear Lord, we thank you for the food on this table and the needs you provide for daily. Your blessings are graciously received. Amen."

A barely audible chorus of amens echoed.

"Miguel?" John looked at the young teen expectantly.

He huffed but put his tablet down. No electronics at the table wasn't an official rule but fell under the *respect others* umbrella.

I grinned at him and passed him the bowl of rolls. "Maybe after dinner you can help me."

His gaze washed over me in speculation. "With what?"

Good question. I didn't actually *need* Miguel's help —the challenge list Amanda had written out was a good framework, saving me time trying to figure out content to post, but unlike most of the other boys I could connect with over football or other sports, I found myself outside the walls Miguel had erected around himself.

"I'm supposed to beef up my online presence."

"I saw that pregame video you posted on Sunday." John speared a potato with the serving fork and moved the tender spud to his plate. "Especially like how you found the corpsman there to hold and display the flag during the national anthem and then you guys did the twenty-two push up challenge together." He grinned at me as he passed the roast dish to Trey. "Tell me, did you let him beat you, or do you need to spend some extra hours at the gym this week?"

"Ah, snap." Mason flicked his fingers.

I held up my hands. "We'll never know, will we?"

"Bruh, he should do a TikTok challenge." Trey's eyes widened with excitement.

I picked up my fork. "You mean one of those things your generation does that gets us impossible-to-open laundry detergent containers?"

Mason snorted. "Says the guy from the generation probably responsible for warning labels on five-gallon buckets."

I pointed the utensil in my hand at Mason. "Touché."

"Naw, not like that," Trey said around a mouthful of food. He swallowed. "How are your dance moves?"

"Umm."

"The Renegade?" Mason asked.

"What's the Renegade?" John looked between the two teens.

At least I wasn't the only one clueless about the current trends.

Trey waved a hand. "Just a dance some fourteen-year-old created. You *are* better than a fourteen-year-old, aren't you, Peter?"

With that kind of taunting? "At dancing? Not a chance."

"Not the Renegade." Miguel entered the conversation for the first time.

Mason folded his arms. "What do you suggest then?"

Miguel stared at me. Took my measure. "Flip the Switch challenge."

"But that's for couples, bruh," Trey whined.

Miguel cut him a look. "It's for two people, dipwad."

"Miguel." John spoke in censure.

"What's the Flip the Switch challenge?" I asked, hoping to defuse anything wanting to ignite.

"You dance to Drake's song "Nonstop" while someone stands next to you. The light switch gets switched off, and when it's turned back on, you and the other person have reversed positions and clothes," Mason supplied.

I looked at Miguel. On the surface, the challenge didn't seem like much. Not very interesting, entertaining, or embarrassing for me. A prank wasn't even involved. Why did he want me to this challenge specifically?

"Who would I trade places with?" He said the challenge was for couples. Would Amanda—

"Trey." Miguel pointed.

Trey blinked. "Me? Why me?"

I studied Trey. We had the same light shade of brown hair. His eyes were also brown, while mine were...well, whatever color they decided to be in the moment. The rest of our features weren't too similar, but—I scanned the occupants sitting around the table —we looked the most alike of anyone else here.

Miguel's brow rose in a challenge.

He didn't just want me to participate in a TikTok hashtag. He wanted me to make a statement.

John cleared his throat, obviously having worked it out too. "I'm not sure—"

"You've never told anyone about us. About your *home*." His lips curled. "In all your interviews, not a single word. You think you're better than us, now that you have money and fame, but we know where you came from." He made a scoffing noise. "Mason sleeps on the same lumpy bed you did, although not for much longer."

"Miguel." John spoke in a warning tone.

"Naw, man." Miguel stood and threw down his napkin. "I'm not going to help you when you haven't done anything to help us but throw a football. Like that's going to do any good." He swiped his tablet and stalked out of the dining room.

I blinked at the kid's retreating back. Was that how he saw things? I did tend to keep my past private, not wanting the media to eat it up like they were somehow entitled to the hardships I'd endured. I didn't want my story to become the next block-buster hit. But I'd *never* turn my back on the kids at Boys to Men or any like them. Contrary to Miguel's accusations, I hadn't forgotten where I'd come from or the people who'd helped me get to where I was now.

"Wow." Trey broke the silence. "I didn't know he could say so many words all together at one time."

"Should I talk to him?" I hooked my thumb over my shoulder, addressing the question to John.

John wiped his mouth. "Give him a few minutes. And maybe yourself too. You're going to have to know how to give him a real answer when you talk to him. The baloney radar is keen with that one."

We finished the meal with the banter, snark, and attitude I expected from the guys. John excused himself to take Miguel's half-eaten plate to him in his room.

"Guess we're on cleanup duty." I stacked empty plates.

"I, uh, got algebra homework." Trey dashed down the hall.

"You going to ditch me too?" I asked Mason.

He picked up the roast pan in one hand and the salad bowl in the other. "Now, I wouldn't do you like that."

The two of us made quick work of clearing the table.

"So." I opened the dishwasher. "You've got a big birthday coming up."

He ran a plate under the faucet spray and handed it to me to load. "Yeah."

"Any plans?"

He shrugged. Turning eighteen was a milestone for any kid, but not always the easiest for those in the system. Aging out could be scary. Almost like a fledgling bird being kicked out of the nest and expected to soar when he didn't even know how to flap his wings.

I dried my hands on a dishtowel, then pulled an envelope out of my back pocket. "Here. An early birthday present."

He wiped his hands on his jeans. "You didn't have to. Should I open it now or what?'

"Go ahead and open it."

His fingers slid under the flap and ripped the envelope's top. He pulled out a single sheet of paper, his eyes tracking each line as he read.

He looked up at me. "Are you serious?"

I'd been in his position before. Felt like everyone

else had gotten a head start because they'd come from a two-parent home when I hadn't. Or they'd had a chance to go to a private school while my education happened within the walls of a Title I school. Or any number of other privileges it seemed others took for granted, which had propelled them forward while I'd felt as if someone were physically holding me back. If it hadn't been for my athletic ability…

Well, I didn't want the kids at Boys to Men to feel like they didn't have choices or couldn't make something of themselves, and I was in a unique position to kind of push them in life's race, so to speak.

"I'm serious. I don't want you to think you don't have options or no one is in your corner."

Mason's wrist went limp, the paper threatening to float to the floor. "A full scholarship? For real?"

I smiled. "John says you're really talented at fixing cats. There's a Universal Technical Institute in both Long Beach and Rancho Cucamonga, or if there's something else you'd rather pursue at a traditional university…" I leaned back against the counter. "You can be anything you want to be, Mason."

He looked at the paper, belief slowly sinking in. "Miguel was *so* wrong about you."

I laughed. "He was right in that I don't share my past with the press."

"Why not?"

"I've tried to keep my life on and off the field separate, although that's not working so much anymore.

Also, I think I was trying to protect you guys. I didn't want to turn John and all of you into a feel-good Sunday special."

"But don't you realize the platform you have?" Miguel's voice surprised me. I hadn't known he was listening. "You've got a voice people will listen to, but you aren't saying anything, man. When people see you, especially in your jersey, they automatically respect you. But Trey here—" He flung his arm out to point to Trey, who stepped out from behind a wall. "People take one look at him and lock their car doors before speeding past. The Flip the Switch challenge might open some people's eyes to the judgments they jump to right off the bat."

Trey shrugged. "I'm game if you are."

I clapped them both on the shoulders. "Let's go make a video."

@PeterReynolds

#mycausemycleats is coming up and I'm excited to share both the design and a cause I'm passionate about for a personal reason.

AMANDA

I glanced around the living room one more time to make sure I had everything I needed for the next few hours before I sank into my couch with a Sherpa blankie, my bowl of extra-butter popcorn, and the last three episodes of Grey's Anatomy.

Snacks, check.

Warmth, check.

Remote, check.

One last trip to the bathroom to empty my bladder, then I could ignore reality and get lost in a world of dreamy doctors and their complicated love lives. I snickered as I remembered the elbow jab I'd given Molly the first time Ben showed up on the scene. Who would have imagined our very own McDreamy would join our ranks? Or two, rather, as Nicole had managed to snag her own sexy doctor.

I flushed the toilet and washed my hands before pattering back to the main room. Picking up the remote, I settled into my favorite corner of the sofa. There. Only thing left—turning on the episode...

My phone trilled on the coffee table.

I sighed and exchanged the remote for my cell, pausing at my sister's name on the screen. Whereas the rest of my family had written me off, opting for "tough love" and "not answering my cry for attention," my sister Stella still checked in and had become the lone thread connecting me with the other members of my family. Without her, I'd never have known Dad had gotten the promotion he'd been gunning for the past six months. Or that my niece had made the dean's list for the second time in a row. Or that my brother had had a cancer scare.

Stella's calls came with a price tag though. While she wasn't willing to cut me out of her life until I "stopped playing the sympathy card," she subscribed to the rest of my family's belief that I was simply a hypochondriac and my symptoms were psychosomatic. After catching me up on family news, Stella would not-so-subtly share a medical study she just happened upon along with the name and contact info of a local counselor or therapist.

I was tempted to ignore the ringing and jump into my escape at Grey Sloan Memorial Hospital, but Charles, my brother, had gone to a follow-up with his primary care doctor, and I wanted to make sure the final test results had come back confirming good news.

Tapping on the screen, I pulled the phone to my ear. "Hi, Stella. How's it going?"

"Oh, I'm glad you answered."

That put me on alert, and I sat up straighter. "Why? What's up?"

She laughed away the concern in my voice. "Nothing. It's just you ignore my calls more than you answer, so I'm glad to actually be talking to you."

My spine lost some of its rigidness. "Right. How'd Charles's appointment go?"

She filled me in on the details, confirming the scare had been just that and we didn't have any reason to be worried anymore.

"That's great." I traced the triangle play button on the remote. "Hey, I hate to cut this short—" Actually, that was exactly what I hoped to do. Maybe save myself a repeat lecture about ending my charade and patching things up with the rest of the family. "—but I should probably get—"

"Did you call Dr. Thompson yet?"

Dr. Thompson was the psychiatrist Stella most often urged me to see.

"I don't want to spend another holiday season with your spot at the table empty, Amanda."

Acid churned in my stomach. I knew my parents and siblings blamed me for my absence at family gatherings and holidays, but I hadn't been invited to any of those events in years. It was a unique kind of hurt, your family's rejection.

My nose stung as tears threatened to build. "I've got to go, Stell-Belle. Thanks for the update on Charles. Give Danielle a kiss from her Aunt Mandy." I sniffed and ended the call.

You're not crazy, I told myself for the thousandth time. However, the conviction of the claim was losing weight. What if Delores really was just a figment of my imagination?

Your imagination can't spike your body temperature. Your imagination can't cause bone-deep pain. Your imagination, no matter how great, can't create real physical effects or alter your lab work.

But it could make me doubt my own sanity at times.

Okay, enough reality. Time for an escape. I pushed the play button harder than necessary, and the opening song, scene sequence, and credits ran on the TV. Just as the last notes ended, a knock sounded on the door.

"You have *got* to be kidding me." Couldn't a girl binge-watch her favorite show without any interruptions?

With a huff, I threw off the blanket and stomped to the door. Yanking it open, I blinked in surprise at Jocelyn and Malachi on the other side.

"What are you two doing here?"

Malachi removed his cowboy hat while Jocelyn's lips quirked. "Nice to see you too. Can we come in?"

She looked over my shoulder into the apartment, curiosity making her eyes gleam.

Though they were my best friends, my sewing girls had never been to my home. Secrets were easier kept when not inviting people *too* close. One look in the kitchen cabinet two doors to the left of the sink would reveal multiple prescription bottles that would surely raise a plethora of questions.

That's right. I kept my medication in the kitchen instead of the medicine cabinet in the bathroom because, ew, who wanted to down pills beside the toilet?

Of course, barring Jocelyn and her boyfriend from entering would also raise questions. I opened the door wider and stepped out of the way.

Jocelyn wrapped me in a hug as she passed. "It's good to see you again."

I scurried into the living room and picked up the empty soda can on the coffee table, retreating to the kitchen to toss the aluminum into the recycling bin. "Can I get you guys something to drink?"

I really was happy to see Jocelyn. Ever since she'd moved to be closer to Malachi, a screen and video calls had kept us connected. I'd gladly postpone my TV date with Doctor Dreamy to hang out with her...but I also had to make sure she stayed away from the second cabinet to the left of the sink in the kitchen.

"I'm fine, thank you." Malachi's baritone carried through to the kitchen.

"I'll take some water," Jocelyn said. "But I can get it myself." She stepped into the small kitchen, hand reaching for the bronze pull of the cabinetry.

I practically lunged in front of her, blocking her from what sat behind door number one. My lips obeyed the command to smile, but the effort didn't keep Jocelyn's brow from folding.

"You're a guest. I'll get it for you."

Her arms crossed. "Guest, huh?"

I slipped a hand behind the cabinet door directly to the left of the sink and pulled out a glass. "Only since this is the first time you've been here." The apartment had come with a double osmosis water filter, so I filled her cup from the tap.

She looked around the kitchen, then accepted the full glass I held out to her. "I wonder why that is," she mumbled before taking a drink.

Another knock sounded from my front door.

Who now?

I shepherded Jocelyn from the kitchen, then crossed to the door and opened it. Nicole, Drew, and Betsy smiled back at me. Well, Nicole and Drew smiled. Betsy maintained her usual unimpressed, almost annoyed expression.

"Um, hi?" What were the odds of three out of four of my best friends plus their significant others all descending upon my door unannounced at relatively the same time being completely coincidental?

Yeah, I didn't think so either.

Betsy breezed past me without a word, stopping in the middle of the living room and circling slowly.

"Can we come in?" Nicole asked, pointing inside.

I stepped back. "Of course."

Nicole and Drew greeted Jocelyn and Malachi with smiles and hugs. I looked between them then peeked my head over the threshold to peer down the hall. Empty.

"Should I leave the door open for Molly and Ben?" I asked with a slight *this is funny but not really* tone to my voice.

Nicole laughed. "Probably a good idea. They were pulling up about the time we entered the building."

Sure enough, a minute later my friend and her new husband strolled up the hall hand in hand.

"Come on in. Join the party," I quipped.

Molly ducked her head, hiding the guilty blush that stained her cheeks.

I closed the door behind them and leaned against the wood. My small apartment could barely contain the onslaught of all my friends at once. I had seating for three, maybe four if everyone smooshed on the couch—which seemed to be the case as Ben settled in beside Malachi, a hand on Molly's hip helping her balance on his lap. Drew and Nicole had taken up posts perching on the sofa's arms. Betsy stayed standing as central as possible, looking around with a critical eye.

I pushed off the door and tentatively entered the midst of my friends. "So, what brings all of you by?"

That's right, Amanda. Keep your voice chipper. Don't let them suspect you have anything to hide.

Well, above whatever it was they already suspected that had brought them swarming in numbers.

"You know, I'm kind of disappointed," Betsy said, surprising me. Her disappointment needed so many reinforcements?

"I kind of always figured you'd never invited us over because you were hiding something."

My breath caught in my throat.

"I thought maybe you were secretly a hoarder and didn't want us to witness your collection of used toothbrushes you couldn't bring yourself to throw away or whatever."

I exhaled. "Nope. As you can see, not a hoarder."

It was frightening, Betsy's ability to narrow her eyes and look at a person as if she could peel back the layers and peer into the heart.

I clasped my hands behind my back so she couldn't see their fidgeting.

"No one really thought that." Nicole shook her head. "But something *is* going on, isn't it? At first, we thought it must be work—especially everything that went on with the Stampeders. But you've been transferred, and things seemed to have settled."

"We're just worried about you," Molly picked up, tag-teaming their concern. "You've seemed…distant. You're missing out on things. Canceling plans. Being vague."

"You're flaking out again."

Leave it to Betsy to speak bluntly.

Jocelyn scooted to the edge of the couch cushion. "We want to help. Whatever it is and in whatever way possible. We're friends and we just want to be there for you."

"So…" Nicole drawled out. "Is there anything you want to tell us? Anything we can help with?"

The guys had been quiet. Silently supporting their women as my friends attempted to support me. Seven pairs of eyes stared back at me expectantly. Open. Free of judgement. Free of pity. Free of shame.

If I told them about Delores, would that change? And what of Ben and Drew? They were doctors, but would their profession more quickly rob my friends of their good regard for me and my sanity, or could they actually help?

I wanted to tell them. Hiding this secret, pretending to be or feel something I wasn't, ate away at me. But my own family had turned their backs on me when I'd come to them and needed them. If I told my friends and their response was the same as other people who were supposed to be the closest to me…

Then I really would be utterly alone.

I didn't think I could bear it.

I pushed down the guilt, not willing to take the risk.

"Amanda," Molly pleaded. "Whatever it is, please tell us."

They had all gathered as a sort of intervention

because they knew something was up. I had to throw them a bone, but what?

Another knock sounded on my door. All my friends were already here. Who could it be now?

@AmandaMurphy

"A day without a friend is like a pot without a single drop of honey." Wise words from Winnie the Pooh.

I had the video of the Flip the Switch challenge all ready to go. With a click of a button, the short reel of Trey and me would be uploaded onto multiple platforms. I had to say, the few seconds—even without any words spoken—were compelling. Anyone willing to look a layer deeper than the surface could see the heart of the matter. Trey looked much as I had as a teen, anger and hurt over the lot life had handed him shadowing the light usually found in youth's eyes. Jaded skepticism carving grooves and hardening features which should still be soft with innocence.

Trey had worn a pair of oversized jeans slung extra low on his narrow hips as well as a baggy black T-shirt. I was thankful for the larger clothes, since I had an extra hundred pounds on the teen, easy. But we hadn't gone looking for anything special. The shirt and pants had come from his own dresser drawer.

As for me, I'd driven home to retrieve a jersey. The material ended up swallowing Trey's frame, but the image lent a *look what he could grow into* type of vibe.

The boys had helped come up with a caption to go with the video, but I'd promised Amanda not to post anything without her approval. Plus, her expertise on reaching more viewers would be appreciated as well.

Which was why, after I'd left Trey and Miguel at Boys to Men, I'd driven straight to Amanda's apartment and perhaps knocked with a little more enthusiasm than needed. The video would be the opening of a door. I'd been in the business long enough to know reporters would be cornering me for interviews about my past and upbringing after this. But maybe more than one door could be opened. Maybe Amanda could see the benefits and inspiration *she* could be if she became a little more transparent with people as well.

The literal door made of wood and paint opened in front of me, a wide-eyed Amanda looking a bit like a cornered animal on the other side. I gazed past her into her apartment and saw the place packed with people. I'd definitely walked in on something.

I rocked my weight back on my heels. "If now is a bad time, I can come back later."

Amanda's blue eyes lost focus for half a second before snapping up to drill into mine. Her hand reached out and hooked around my arm, hauling me into her home.

Okay, she wasn't big enough or strong enough to physically force me anywhere I didn't want to go. And as she was drawing me closer to her side, who was I to protest?

She closed the door behind us, then wrapped her arm around my waist. She looked up at me, her expression silently pleading for me to go along with whatever scheme she had going on.

Amanda had essentially called an audible. If I was going to convince her I was on her team, then I'd need to prove I had her back.

She must have seen my agreement written on my face, because the tight lines around her mouth softened. She turned back toward the people who were watching us as closely as refs on a scoring play.

Amanda tilted her head, resting her temple against my ribs. Her hand came up, fingers splaying across my stomach.

My abs quivered under her touch. I could bench press two hundred pounds without a twinge, but one touch from Amanda made my muscles turn to Jell-O.

The man perched on the sofa's arm rose. He stared at me, recognition dropping his jaw.

"That's Peter Reynolds." He pointed, then turned back to the others and repeated himself. "That's Peter Reynolds."

"Oh…" The small woman on the lap of one of the other guys pulled the word out into three syllables.

"Peter and I have been rekindling our relationship. If things have seemed…off…with me, it's just the, uh, blooming of something new." Amanda flicked her gaze back up at me, her breath held captive with how still she'd become.

So that was the game afoot. A fake play of diversion. Again, who was I to protest?

In answer, I wrapped my arm around Amanda's shoulder and drew her even closer to my side. Her body sagged into me, and my ribcage expanded with the knowledge she was letting me help her in some small way.

Even if the help came in the form of deceiving apparently concerned friends.

One step at a time, I reminded myself. Her trust needed to be earned somewhere.

"Care to introduce me to your friends, sweetheart?" I trailed my fingers down Amanda's arm in a languid path, making them retreat the way they'd come when they reached her elbow. Tiny bumps rose on her skin, and I suppressed a satisfied smile.

Amanda may excel at pretending one thing when the other was true, but her body betrayed her. She was not as immune to me as she liked to let on.

And seeing as my job at the moment was to act the doting boyfriend, maybe I could blur the lines between pretend and reality, if only for a little while.

"The guy practically salivating on himself there is Drew Bauer."

I offered my free hand to Drew, not willing to loosen my hold on Amanda for a second. What kind of fake boyfriend would I be if I did that?

Drew shook my hand, looking back at the woman sitting askance on the other couch arm. His grin turned goofy. "It's Peter Reynolds."

The woman shook her head but laughed. She stood and rounded the coffee table. "I'm Nicole." She smiled at me. "Drew, if you don't stop looking at him like that, I'm going to get jealous."

Immediately Drew's attention snapped to Nicole. His eyes darkened, and the grin he gave her turned wolfish. As if he'd like nothing better than to find a private corner to show her just how much she never needed to worry or have a reason to be jealous.

"Moving on." Amanda's voice held a smile. "Next we have Malachi and Jocelyn."

The man in a western-style button-up stood, his grip firm and full of calluses. In a contest of strength, I wouldn't want to go up against him. Throwing bales of hay and punching cattle just may be more of a workout than kettle bars and battling ropes.

"It's nice to meet you, Peter," Jocelyn said kindly.

"Nice to meet you too."

"This is Ben, Molly, and Betsy.' Amanda pointed to each person in turn.

"Great job against the Mustangs on Sunday," Ben said.

"They're a great team to play against. Keep us on our toes."

Loud whispers came from the opposite end of the couch. I turned my head to see Nicole and Drew in some kind of debate. In a huff, Nicole threw up her hands. Drew kissed her cheek.

"Don't pay them any attention." The only one not coupled up, Betsy, rolled her eyes. "They're always squabbling about something, then making up in some public display or another." She jutted her chin at them. "Get a room."

"Gladly," Drew replied, nuzzling Nicole's neck.

"So, how long have you guys been back together?" Molly asked.

Back together. Meaning Amanda had shared our past relationship with her friends. What had she told them? What reason had she given for our breaking up?

I looked to Amanda to answer. She was the play caller in this game.

Amanda's smile wobbled. "Shortly after being transferred from the Stampeders to the Condors. Peter couldn't resist me." She shimmied her shoulders to show she was teasing.

I pulled her in front of me and draped my arms over her shoulders, crisscrossing my forearms across her chest, then cupping my hands on her deltoids. I dropped my chin to the top of her head. "That's the truth. I never could resist Amanda."

Betsy snorted. "I don't see why not."

"Hey!" Amanda protested, but I pulled her more firmly to my chest.

"Well, I'm happy for you." Jocelyn reached up under her headwrap to scratch an itch. "And relieved. We were really worried about you when you kept canceling on us."

Amanda stiffened so slightly I doubted anyone noticed. I slowly rocked us side to side with small movements.

"I'm fine." Amanda's voice was tight.

"And I apologize if I've been monopolizing her time and taking her away from you guys." With my nose only inches away from Amanda's hair, her citrus-scented shampoo teased my senses. I inhaled deeply before continuing. "Let me make it up to you all. I know she'll be at the game this Sunday. I can get tickets for the rest of you, and you can all hang out and enjoy the game on me. What do you say?"

"Yes!" Drew shouted. He shrugged his shoulders when everyone laughed at him. "What? Tickets are hard to come by." He grinned at me. "I know Nicole and I will forgive you even quicker if we can get an extra ticket for her daughter, Sierra, and if you can somehow work it out that she can meet Grant Hawthorne. Sierra is the quarterback of her youth football team and would love to meet the Condors' QB."

"Drew," Nicole hissed.

"It's okay," I assured her. "I'll see what I can do about Grant, but of course we couldn't leave another star player out of the game."

"That's really nice of you," Molly said.

I blamed Amanda's intoxicating scent and the mesmerizing feel of her skin beneath my palm for what I did and said next. But could a guy really be blamed for wanting to hold on to his heart's desire for a little while longer?

"Hopefully my bribe has bought me enough good-will to steal more of Amanda's time later this week."

Amanda lifted her hands to clasp my arms where they crossed over her chest. She curled her fingernails into my skin. Enough to nip, but not enough to bite.

"What's later this week?" she asked.

"You remember, don't you, sweetheart? You talked me into accepting the invitation to the gala benefiting Social Advocates for Youth."

"You donate to SAY?" Nicole straightened.

Betsy snapped her fingers. "Down girl."

"Of course Amanda will go with you." Jocelyn waved her hand. "Now that we know the only thing she was hiding was a man, we won't worry about her so much."

"A man just means you should worry more," Betsy mumbled.

Everyone chimed in with their opinion on whether a man in a woman's life meant more or less worry.

Amanda turned her head to whisper into my ear. "Thank you for pretending to be interested in me again."

I pulled back enough to look into her eyes. "Who said I was pretending?"

@CondorsOfficial

Help us wish @JebAbeson a happy birthday!

13

AMANDA

"You look amazing in that dress." Molly sat on my bed eyeing me with friendly appreciation.

Of their own accord, my hands ran across my stomach and down my hips, the small sequins sewn into the lace overlay of the form-fitting gown rough against my palm.

Nicole stood near the door of my small walk-in closet munching on green nori sheets, while Betsy leaned a hip against my dresser. Jocelyn and Malachi had returned to the ranch but planned on driving back down over the weekend to attend the football game.

My three friends looked at me expectantly, no doubt waiting for a reply. "Umm…thanks."

"He's either tamed her or broken her." Betsy inspected her nails. "Either way, I'm not sure I approve of the change."

I looked at Betsy askance. "What are you talking about?"

"I don't get the appeal of athletes personally—"

"Peter Reynolds is to sports as Adam Levine is to music," Nicole interjected.

Betsy gave her a look. The kind that reminded everyone in the room that she was immune to musicians. And more than that, of her number one rule: never date a musician. Set into place as a backup in case the immunity wore off.

"As I was saying," Betsy continued as if Nicole hadn't spoken, "I don't get the appeal myself, but Peter totally seems your type."

"And?" Molly asked.

Betsy threw out her hands like the answer was obvious. "And she hasn't made a single shocking declaration. By this time, I'd expected to hear all about his broad shoulders and the way those tight pants, or whatever they're called, make his *el pompis*"—she smacked her backside—"look good on the pitch."

I looked up at the ceiling, down the far wall, across the floor. I'd heard the ridiculousness come out of my own mouth before, but somehow, hearing someone else say the same things seemed all the more embarrassing.

"That just goes to show how much she actually likes Peter," Molly argued. "She's not pretending or playing around with him."

My eyes slid shut, but I couldn't unhear the words.

Who said I was pretending? Peter's voice, his question, had kept me up at night. If it weren't for the fact he'd put me in a corner—

Don't blame him. You did this to yourself, my conscience interrupted. Pesky thing, consciences. They kept you up at night too.

Anyway, if it weren't for being in a corner—no matter who'd put me here—I would've called Peter and told him I couldn't go with him to the gala. But he'd "invited" me in front of my friends, who all thought we were dating and who had graciously decided to turn sewing night into help-Amanda-get-ready night. If I canceled, they'd want to know why, and I couldn't tell them why without telling them Peter and I weren't really dating, and I couldn't tell them why I'd lied to them about that without also confessing my harbored secret about Delores.

I put a hand to my head. Just following the thread of my deceit was exhausting.

My chest tightened, but I knew I couldn't blame Delores for this particular discomfort. It was the weight of my guilt crushing me.

The truth will set you free.

I opened my mouth, but no sound emerged. As if the truth were too big to pass through my windpipe.

Molly scooted off the bed. "Come on. I'll help with curling your hair."

Because she was a good friend, not because she knew my arms would get tired before I even made it halfway around my head. Like a coward, I let the opportunity to fess up pass me by and followed Molly into the bathroom with my chin tucked to my chest.

Twenty minutes later, my long hair cascaded down my back in shiny waves as Nicole put the finishing touches on my makeup. I stared at my reflection in the mirror, surprised to see me staring back. After applying eye liner and blush and other products I never wore and didn't know the names of, and taming my hair into a hairstyle I'd never waste time on day-to-day, I'd half expected not to recognize my reflection. But there I was. Still me, but a more refined and classier version.

It doesn't matter what he thinks, I chided myself. I'd untangled our lives once before for his sake, but I didn't think I had the strength or fortitude to do it again. So, for Peter's sake, I had to make sure we kept our distance. And I somehow had to convince him of the wisdom of the separation.

And maybe remind myself while I was at it.

The curtains on my windows were all open to let in the light, which was why I noticed Peter's Ford pickup turn the corner, looking for a parking spot.

I grabbed my phone off the dresser and sent a quick text to let him know I'd be out in a second. If he came in, I'd have to keep up the charade of our budding romance in front of Molly, Nicole, and Betsy, and that thought made me want to crawl under my covers and shut out the world.

"Peter just pulled up, so I'm going to head out," I told my friends.

"I'm not one to be old-fashioned," Nicole tsked, "but shouldn't he pick you up at the door instead of honking and expecting you to run out to him?"

"He's not honking," I rushed to assure her. Every minute I stood talking to them was another minute Peter would use to find a place to park and head off my quick escape.

My phone buzzed in my hand, and I quickly glanced down. Peter had answered my text.

Peter: Umm…???

My brows furrowed. Why was he confused? I'd said I'd be out in a second. My gaze rose and my jaw dropped as I read the letters of the text I'd sent.

Amanda: Be out in sex.

Stupid autocorrect! My thumbs flew over the keyboard on the screen to fix my fat-finger blunder, and I hit send on a rush of breath.

Then choked on an inhale as I realized autocorrect had struck again.

Amanda: I meant, be out for sex.

"No. No. No. No. In a sec! I meant be out in a second!"

"What's wrong?" Molly asked.

Betsy snatched my phone out of my hand. I made a grab for it but only got a fistful of air for my efforts.

Betsy smirked. "Maybe she's not broken after all.

Course, I always thought you were all talk with no follow through. Guess I was wrong."

"It's a typo! Autocorrect hates me." I let my weight pull me onto my bed, not caring if I wrinkled my dress.

Molly and Nicole huddled by Betsy so they could read the screen too. Molly hid a snicker behind her hand.

"Kill me now." I pulled a pillow toward me to hide my face.

"None of that." Nicole intercepted the pillow, then prodded me in the side. "We've all got an embarrassing autocorrect story. Peter seems like the kind of guy who'll laugh this off, not take you up on your offer." She didn't successfully hide her smile.

A knock on the front door echoed through my apartment.

"I'd open the door, but now I'm afraid for my virtue," Betsy teased.

I threw the pillow at her, which she caught with a laugh.

Another knock.

Nicole, Molly, and Betsy stared at me. Betsy startled, then looked down at my phone, still in her hand. She grinned, tossing me the device.

"Looks like he texted back."

Peter: I'm saving myself for marriage, but if that's on the table...

I covered my hot cheeks with my hand. This was not good. Of course, I knew he was kidding, but he was also flirting. And more than that, my traitorous body *liked* it. Unlike when Delores made my heart beat out of rhythm and caused my chest to hurt, my heart now seemed to pump stronger, and the fluttery sensation against my breastbone caused pleasant tingles to radiate between my ribs.

No, no, no, no, I repeated, this time in my mind.

Peter: I'm kidding. I'm guessing autocorrect was messing with you?

"Are you going to keep him out there all night?" Nicole asked with a frown.

I sighed and dragged my body off the bed. My steps were heavy as I trudged toward the front door, my friends following behind.

I took a steadying breath as I turned the doorknob. *You're doing the right thing. The selfless thing.* Putting Peter's needs above my own was the only way I'd allowed myself to express my love.

Because, yeah, I'd never stopped loving this man.

"Wow," he said in quiet awe when the door swung open. "You look...wow."

My fingers found their way into the folds of material along the sides of my legs. I couldn't look up at him, afraid he'd see my struggle before I could once again lock my feelings away into a safe spot. Away from any prying eyes. Especially his.

A warm finger crooked under my chin, gentle pressure raising my face until I had no choice but to meet Peter's eyes. They were a deep green—like a pine tree, which reminded me of Christmas morning and crackling fires and snuggling up under a cozy blanket. Like coming home and finding a place to belong. A person to belong to.

"There you are," he said softly, and I wondered if he meant more than just meeting my gaze—if he could actually see through the windows of my irises to my very soul.

"Here, let me see your phone, and I'll take your picture," Molly offered.

I was glad she'd spoken and broken the bubble that had momentarily captured Peter and me in its sphere.

Liar.

I turned from Peter to face Molly and the other two ladies. "It's not prom."

Molly looked at me funny. "I just thought you'd want a picture to post to social media."

Oh. Right. That would be something I'd normally do.

Peter put his arm around my shoulder and pulled me into his side. I tried to shallow my breathing so I wouldn't get a heady whiff of his spicy cologne. Attempted to ignore how soft the fabric of his evening coat was and how, when I leaned against him, I felt stronger than I did when I was alone. My smile wobbled, and I mentally put pins in the corners to stake the edges in their properly happy place.

"There." Molly lowered my phone. "You two are so adorable together."

I took the phone and stuffed it into my handbag. After saying our goodbyes to the girls, Peter threaded his fingers through mine and tugged me out the door. He led me out of the apartment building but then paused under a street lamp, turning to face me.

"Something wrong?" Besides *this*. Him. Me. Together. If the robot from *Lost in Space* were here, he'd be rolling around with his robotic arms flailing repeating *Danger!* over and over again.

"No. I just wanted to look at you again."

My cheeks flushed, and though I'd done a good job of avoiding it until then, I allowed myself to look at Peter for the first time that night. *Danger! Danger!* The robotic voice squealed in my mind. Looking that good in a tux should be illegal. James Bond who? 007 couldn't cut near the figure Peter did in his tailored suit. The lines of his evening wear broadened his shoulders and tapered at his trim waist. My heart, caged in my chest, beat against the bars of my ribs.

Peter opened the passenger door for me and helped me climb into his truck. It only took a short while before we reached the convention center where the gala was being held. Just enough time to rein my pulse in and give myself a stern talking to.

"Before we go in, I want to show you something." Peter turned off the truck engine, then rotated in his seat to face me. He fiddled with his phone before handing the cell to me. "This was why I stopped by your place the other day."

I watched the short video of Peter and a teen switching places, clothes, and posture. The piece, obviously shot for TikTok, was powerful. Social media may often get a bad rap, but used intentionally, could be a platform and catalyst for much needed awareness and change. Some people may view Peter's video and receive only entertainment at watching the hulking defensive player squeeze his massive body into clothes made for someone much smaller, but other people wouldn't miss the unspoken message—not to judge or label a youth based on looks or upbringing. That, given an opportunity, they could grow up into someone worthy of the title "role model."

I brushed a rebellious tear away. "This is great, Peter."

He took back his phone and tapped a few times before handing it back to me. "This is the caption we came up with to go along with the video. What do you think?"

I haven't shared my past with the media for multiple reasons, wanting my actions on the field to speak for themselves. But recently I've been challenged to embrace the journey I've traveled to maybe help and encourage those who are on a similar road. I was the foster kid no one wanted.

Always acting out and getting into trouble until my last option came in the form of a group home for difficult boys. I remember people calling me a hooligan. A gangster. No good and would never amount to anything. That my future would be behind bars. Most of these comments came from people who didn't know me. Who judged me with a single look. Only one man seemed to look at me and see potential. John Allen, founder and operator of Boys to Men, the group home I spent the majority of my teen years in. If not for him, I wouldn't be where I am today. #ShowLoveNotHate #JudgeNot #BeTheDifference

My eyes rose to meet Peter's. His face swam a bit as I blinked back more tears. "You're going to post this?"

"Someone challenged me to use my voice to inspire others. I'm not sure how much I can actually do that, but I'm willing to try if it means I can help someone else."

His expression remained open, almost an invitation. That someone had been me, and he'd turned the tables on that challenge. He wanted me to follow in his footsteps. Strip away the pretense.

If only I could.

I handed his phone back and slid my gaze to the side. "This is amazing." I forced myself to look at him a moment more. "*You're* amazing."

He smiled, though the gesture hinted at a degree of sadness. "Ready to go in?"

I nodded, and he exited the truck, rushing around the front to get to my door before I could open it myself. He offered me his elbow, and I threaded my arm through his.

The convention center had been decked out with elaborate floral arrangements and ambient lighting. Men ambled around in tuxedos while women wore glittering gowns and expensive jewelry. I hesitated, feeling out of place.

Peter put a hand to my lower back. "I promise no one will bite."

"Come to these shindigs often, do you?"

He glanced down at me. "No. I usually make it a point not to attend these events."

"Then why—"

"Mr. Reynolds." A middle-aged woman in a silver sheath dress glided toward us, cutting off my question. "We are *so* happy that you decided to accept our invitation. You have no idea how *thrilled* we were to receive your most generous donation. Most generous indeed." She pumped Peter's hand up and down. "The checks that have come in the last few years have been a mystery that we all speculated on. We've been wanting to thank you for *so* long, and now we can. On behalf of all the youth in the city, thank you *so* much."

Peter's neck grew red under his collar. I eyed the woman, then Peter. He mumbled something under his breath as his eyes darted around the room. They settled in a corner. "No thanks necessary. If you'll excuse us, my date was only just mentioning how she could use a refreshment." He practically steered me around the woman to a small bar on the other side of the room.

I laughed. "You face down three-hundred-pound guys who want nothing more than to cream your face in the dirt, but that lady scared you?"

Peter mumbled again.

"What was that? I can't hear you." I cupped my hand around my ear, barely containing my laughter.

He sighed and rubbed the back of his neck. "All my donations have been anonymous before now."

In a day when most people would call a press release for such a thing, Peter had flown under the radar.

"Why?"

"There's a passage in the Bible that talks about giving in secret. To not let even your right hand know what your left hand is doing. I never gave for the recognition or accolades and, quite frankly, receiving that woman's praise and thanks made me uncomfortable."

Peter was not making it easy to dam my feelings for him. "What changed?"

We stepped up to the bar. Peter ordered a ginger ale and I asked for a Shirley Temple. The bartender gave us a funny look but filled our requests.

"Nothing really. I realized the verses in the Bible were warning against appearing righteous for appearance's sake and parading good deeds for the express purpose of receiving earthly honor. That will never be me. I also realized that if I modeled giving—not exactly like the widow woman at the temple who gave all she had, mainly because our circumstances are different—then maybe other people would become aware of the need and seek to fill the gap as well."

The cracked screen. The truck from college he still drove even though he must have received millions of dollars as a signing bonus with the Condors. How big of a gap was Peter single-handedly trying to fill?

All in. As he did everything. He'd embraced his role as a leading figure and sought to be a good example. I was almost afraid he was *too* good a leader, because in that moment, I would have been willing to follow him anywhere.

@DanCush

Keep politics out of sports. Just do your job and catch the pig skin.

@JessSchmidt

@DanCush [Link to article entitled *Why Activist Athletes Are Needed Today More Than Ever*]

14

PETER

As I predicted, the sports journalists latched on to the door to my past that I'd cracked open and attempted to force their way through and examine every crevice and corner. What special angle could they twist that would bring in more viewers than their competition?

The franchise was happy with the extra boost in media attention. More interviews for any of their players meant more air time for their team as well, which somehow converted into more profits.

A one-on-one interview with sports anchorwoman Terri Lang had been set up at the national channel's local headquarters. A nice receptionist welcomed me and showed me back to a room filled with camera equipment, lighting, and more electrical cords than I could count. People with IDs on lanyards around their necks bustled about with urgent senses of purpose, checking equipment and barking orders.

I recognized Terri Lang right away from TV. She had on a checkered pencil skirt, and her shiny black hair was pulled over one of her shoulders. She'd been with the broadcasting company long enough to make a pretty good name for herself, and the fact she was one of the few women in a career dominated by men helped her stand out. She was good at handling athletes, though, and managed to put players at ease and get them to open up where some of her counterparts couldn't. I admired her finesse...when she was handling someone besides me.

I'd have to be careful. She'd even managed to get linebacker Adrian Welzebecker to cry on national television—which had gotten him adoration from fans, as he'd been talking about his high-school sweetheart who was now his wife. But he'd also received some serious ribbing on the practice field and in the locker room.

"Mr. Reynolds." Terri Long strode toward me, her steps purposeful. She held out her hand and gave mine a firm shake. "Thank you so much for joining us." She gave me the rundown of how the interview would go, then asked if I was ready.

"Ready as I'll ever be."

She led me to the stools that had been set up in front of a giant banner with the broadcasting company's logo on it. She sat with the heel of one of her shoes hooked over a rung on the chair and the other planted firmly on the ground. I perched on the edge of my stool, getting as comfortable as I could. The interview wasn't supposed to last more than ten minutes, but I knew that could feel like a lifetime depending on the kind of questions Miss Lang decided to ask.

Someone behind a camera counted us off, holding up fingers and then pointing at Terri.

She smiled that welcoming TV smile that boosted ratings and greeted her viewers through the camera lens.

"We're with Peter Reynolds, defensive end for the Condors." She turned to me. "Thank you for being here, Peter."

I dipped my chin. "Thank you for having me."

Miss Lane folded her hands primly in her lap. "There are so many things we could discuss, what with your impressive record this year and how well your team has been playing overall, but I think our viewers are well aware of these facts. What they may not know and perhaps have been wondering"—she moved her arm in a half circle—"what we all have been wondering, is who is the man behind the jersey?"

I smiled a little and shrugged. "Oh, you know. I'm just a regular guy like everyone else."

She had a tinkling sort of laugh. "Perhaps not so much like everyone else. There aren't many people I know who give away over ninety-percent of their income to charitable causes."

Someone had done some major digging. While I supposed such records were public, the SAY donation had been the first I'd attached my name to. I swallowed and thought quickly about how to respond. "As I said, I'm just a regular guy with regular, everyday needs. The Condors have been more than generous to me, and I've simply allowed that generosity to flow through me to help more people than just myself."

"Speaking of needs..." Terri Lane leaned forward, a look of compassion on her face. "Yours weren't always met growing up, were they? In the past, you've been silent about your years before football, but recently you've let us all see a glimpse of what your early life looked like. In a social media post you shared recently, you said you grew up in a group home. Can you tell us more about that?"

I imagined in editing they'd cut to a picture or even the video of Trey and me. Next time I saw the teen, his head would be too big to fit through a doorway. He had a propensity to show off. All this media attention—his face on national television—would make him preen more than a peacock.

"Mr. Reynolds?" Miss Lane prodded.

I sighed. "My story is one as old as time and all too familiar for too many kids. In my case, my father left the scene early on. So early I don't even remember him. My mother tried the best she could, but life was hard, and she became addicted to substances she claimed made things a little easier. Eventually her addiction led to incarceration and I—an angry, hurting, frightened kid—was put into the system." I shook my head and looked into the camera. "I apologize to the families that took me in early on and tried to make a home for me. You didn't deserve the attitude and defiance I served up."

"A bit difficult, were you?"

"You could say that. So much so that I was eventually sent to John Allen, the founder of Boys to Men. If it weren't for his endurance, patience, and understanding, I'm not sure where I'd be today. John gave me a chance when so many others had turned their backs on me."

"In past interviews, you've alluded to someone who mentored you and instilled the mindset behind your practice of offering a hand to the quarterbacks you sack. Is John Allen that person?"

I nodded. "John taught me that life will constantly knock you down. That I had the choice to get angry about that or to look for someone offering a helping hand up and to be that person to someone else."

"A life lesson we all can reflect on." She shifted her weight on her hip. "Besides the revelation into your past, your recent posts on social media have also led some to speculate about a certain aspect of your present and even possibly your future. Twice now you've posted pictures with a certain woman. Tell us, is anything romantic going on there?"

Once again, the editing crew would probably put up

a side-by-side of the posts with Amanda—the selfie on the plane when we argued about fight songs, and the one the other night leaving for the gala. Amanda would probably watch this, if not for any personal reason then as a member of the team's PR department.

I looked again at the camera and gave what I hoped was a charming smile. "That's a question better asked of the lady."

@AvaWiseman

@PeterReynolds Why the evasive answer to @TerriLang? Are you in a relationship or aren't you?

15

AMANDA

Those pain scales they had in doctor's offices and hospital rooms were deceiving. *From one to ten, what is your pain level?* Well, someone healthy who didn't have a constant companion trying to stage a coup in her body would, on a normal day, say they were at a zero, correct? So if one day they were experiencing something out of the ordinary, a jump to a six or a seven would be cause for concern. (I'm hypothesizing, since I can't recall what being at a zero feels like.) For me, a six is normal. Baseline. What a good day feels like. I am the orange face with lips starting to turn down and eyebrows starting to concave in that worried, icky look.

Today was a good day. I eyed the row of seats matching the row and numbers on our tickets. Thankfully not bleachers, but the pull-down hard plastic wouldn't be comfortable after the long hours of a professional football game. By the time the last whistle blew, I would likely find myself well into the red-faced range of a nine or a ten rating.

"I'm so excited. I've never been to a real live professional game before." Molly barely stopped herself from clapping her hands in excitement.

"Do you even know the rules?" Ben chuckled behind her.

She sniffed. "I've picked up a few things watching Sierra play."

"Yeah, because the NFL is exactly the same as a youth league."

I smirked at Betsy. Her shirt read *My sarcasm is thicker than my thighs.* Probably wore it as an excuse that she'd warned anyone stupid enough to open their mouth in her presence.

Molly hip-checked her. "Sassy pants."

Betsy scooted down the row and unfolded her seat before plopping down. Molly and Ben followed. Sierra was next, but she didn't move, her gaze riveted on a red-and-white-striped bucket with steaming buttered popcorn in the hands of someone farther down the row in front of us.

"Can I have some popcorn? Please, Mom?"

Nicole sucked in her breath. I could practically hear her thoughts. The unhealthy additives. Butter came from an animal and therefore wasn't vegan. Probably some social or environmental issue associated with the favorite snack of millions of Americans.

Jocelyn whispered in my ear. "Which way do you think this will go?"

Drew cleared his throat, arresting Nicole's attention. Some silent communication passed between them before Nicole's bunched shoulders relaxed.

"Sure. And, um, do you want a soda too?" Her voice squeaked at the end, like her throat had tried to close so as not to let the offer out.

Drew wrapped his arms around her and pressed a kiss to her temple. The man had been nothing less than a miracle worker for Nicole and her daughter. If someone had looked up high-strung in the dictionary before Drew came into their lives, a picture of the Applegate ladies would be under the definition. But little by little, Drew had helped to show them that it was okay and even good to loosen up and have fun while they single-handedly tried to save the planet.

Sierra's eyes bugged out. "Really?"

Nicole's lips pressed closed, but she hummed a *mm-hmm* in affirmation.

I leaned toward her. "They have some Hansen's Natural Soda."

Her breath whooshed out, and I chuckled.

"Anyone else want something from the concession stands?" Malachi, ever the gentleman, offered.

Jocelyn pulled him down by his arm and kissed his cheek. "You're so sweet."

The tips of his ears darkened a shade of red, and he

dipped his head, hiding behind the brim of his cowboy hat.

Sweet, shy Malachi.

After everyone started saying things like "Nachos sound good" and "I could go for one of those bratwursts," it was evident Malachi wouldn't be able to carry all the food himself.

Ben stood. "Let me help with the hunting and gathering."

Betsy snorted.

Nicole waved a hand. "Sit down, caveman. I need to go that way anyway."

Drew's eyebrows jumped to his hairline. "Whatever for?"

"Umm…" Nicole's cheeks flushed and her gaze bounced around as if searching for an answer. Finally, she smiled. "The bathroom. You know me. Small bladder."

Drew looked suspicious but didn't say anything. Nicole and Malachi mounted the stairs that led to the landing where souvenir stores, concession stands, and restrooms were offered.

Drew turned to the rest of us. "Was it just me, or was she acting weird?"

"You're talking about Nicole," Betsy said. "Weird is her normal."

"Oh my goodness." Sierra pointed to the field. "Did you see how high that guy jumped?"

Players had filtered onto the field, warming up with

different exercises. A wide receiver practiced vertical jumps in the end zone.

My gaze roamed over the field, seeking a familiar figure. From this distance, I could look my fill without fear of being found out. I was like a kid in a china shop, the admonishment of *look, don't touch* ringing in my ears. Because if I touched, the outcome would be the same as if I'd knocked over fragile porcelain—a million shattered pieces. My heart would be Humpty Dumpty, never able to be put back together again.

Then I spotted him on the sidelines around the twenty-yard mark. Hands on hips, he sank down into a deep lunge, pushed himself up, then sank down again with the opposite leg leading. Instead of the corded earbuds he'd worn on the plane to Salt Lake the week before, a pair of wireless headphones covered his ears. The tune of *Eye of the Tiger* entered my mind, causing my lips to bow.

As if he could feel my gaze on him, Peter looked up. His eyes didn't sweep the stadium, searching. No. He looked up and fastened his attention straight on me much like I imagined a target-seeking missile would.

Locked.

Loaded.

My breath hitched. I fought to tear my gaze away, but then Peter smiled. He lifted his hand and gave me a small wave.

Jocelyn elbowed me playfully. "Looks like he has more on his mind than just the game."

Ignoring her, I waved back, then made a kind of shooing motion. Peter needed to focus. The outcome of the game was too important for his career for him to get distracted.

He grinned as if he knew exactly what I'd been thinking, then continued his lunges down the sidelines.

Malachi and Nicole came back with their arms laden with food, and the field cleared of players, both teams heading to their respective locker rooms to finish getting ready for the game. The stadium filled with spectators ranging from sedate fans in team clothing to those who had painted their bodies and carried large signs in the hopes of attracting the camera people and making it onto the jumbotron. Loud music and fireworks started the event with a bang as the rival teams spilled onto the field.

"This is so exciting." Molly practically shouted over the noise to be heard.

The national anthem played, the coin was tossed, and then the game got underway. The Condors had a nice opening drive, but the other team's defense held the offense at the fifteen-yard line, making it necessary for the kicker to come out and putting three points on the board instead of six.

The whole first half went that way, both teams making little headway as far as scoring was concerned. The points made on both sides had been contributed by the kickers.

"Are games always this…" Jocelyn searched for the right word.

"Boring?" Betsy supplied with an arched brow.

"Long?" Nicole rubbed her palms over the top of her jeans.

"Uneventful?" Molly offered.

Jocelyn laughed. "Yes to all of the above."

"Do we complain when you make us sit through over five hours of the Pride and Prejudice miniseries?" Ben teased.

"Yes!" five female voices exclaimed in unison.

"They aren't wrong." Drew scratched at his jaw, the stubble there longer than usual. Must not have shaved that morning. "You whined more than Chloe when Darcy declared how ardently he loved and admired Lizzie."

Ben groaned. "Don't remind me of the torture."

Molly patted Ben's knee. "It was only fair after you made us sit through all three Godfather movies."

Malachi made a move like he was loosening a tie. "Never let anyone know what you are thinking," he said in his best Al Pacino impersonation.

Jocelyn barked out a laugh. "You would pick that line to quote."

Malachi just smiled.

"I, for one, could have continued with my knowledge of *The Godfather* being limited to what I learned of it from *You've Got Mail*." Molly folded her arms.

Ben kissed the tip of her nose.

Nicole sat up straight. "This is halftime then?" She pointed to the emptying field.

"Ready?" Sierra gripped her mom's hand.

But before Nicole could answer, a voice boomed from the loudspeaker. "The Condors would like to invite Sierra Applegate, Nicole Applegate, and Drew Bauer down to the field."

The jumbotron filled with Drew's surprised face, then panned out to include Sierra and Nicole. They all stood.

"Did you know about this?" Drew whispered.

Nicole reached behind her and grasped Drew's hand as they descended the steps and followed a stadium employee to the entrance to the green. The announcer explained how Drew coached a local youth team and Sierra was the star quarterback. The Condors supported youth sports and loved the opportunity to shine a spotlight on up-and-coming players.

Two more employees waited for the trio on the field. One led Drew to the fifty-yard line while the other accompanied the ladies a few yards down the field. She handed the two Applegate ladies each a ball.

"Nicole is going to throw too?" Jocelyn asked, surprise ticking up her eyebrows.

"Did you know this was going to happen?" Molly pointed her question at me.

I shook my head. I was just as shocked at the events unfolding as any of my other friends.

"I'd suspect Drew of some grand gesture, but he has a seriously confused look on his face," Ben added.

The announcer asked if Sierra was ready, and she nodded. The ball left her hands in a perfect spiral. Drew didn't even have to take a step in order to catch it. He pumped his fist and made to eliminate the distance between them, but the worker in the orange vest stopped him with a hand to his shoulder, pointing down at the football in his hands. He spun the ball, revealing two words painted on the side.

An up-close view on the jumbotron revealed the words—*Will You.*

"Is she…" Even Betsy, uninterested in everything, sat up straighter.

"Will I what?" Drew shouted. The employee had a microphone so we all could hear him over the buzz of the crowd.

Nicole took a deep breath, hiked her arm behind her head, and let her ball fly. It wobbled in the air and didn't have the strength or accuracy Sierra's had. Drew jogged forward and stretched to catch the ball before it hit the ground. He twisted the ball until two more words faced up.

Marry Us?

Everyone seemed to hold their breath.

"Is this really happening?" Jocelyn whispered.

"She's…she's…she's proposing?" Malachi fumbled with words even more than usual.

"But…but…but they haven't been together that long."

Jocelyn laid her head on his shoulder. "You take all the time you need. I'm not going anywhere."

Malachi's cheeks flushed, but he laced his fingers through hers.

"Drew Bauer." Nicole steadily walked toward him. "You are—"

"Yes!" he shouted. The crowd cheered as Drew sprinted forward, wrapped Nicole in his arms, then kissed her for all she was worth.

"I'm going to have to thank him for sparing us all from whatever lovesick speech she had planned." Betsy turned her head from the millions of pixels displaying our friends' affection on the big screen.

Molly shook her head at Betsy.

Ben pulled Molly close, nuzzling her neck. "Still think football is boring?"

She giggled. "No one told me all the points were scored during halftime."

Jocelyn choked on a laugh while Betsy groaned.

@CondorsOfficial

Congratulations to Dr. Drew Bauer and Nicole Applegate on their engagement.

16

PETER

"Great game today, guys." Grant sauntered through the locker room handing out high fives and back slaps. He stopped by me and put a foot up on the bench, leaning forward and resting his forearms on his knees. "How about it, Reynolds? Up for a night out to celebrate?"

I glanced over at him before leaning down to tie my shoe. "Can't. Already have plans."

"Have something to do with the halftime entertainment today? Heard you had a hand in that."

I moved to the other shoe. "Might have. And I need to give my congratulations to the happy couple."

Grant pushed my shoulder. "Why do I feel everything points back to the woman from PR that's been shadowing you? What's her name again?"

"Amanda." I pulled the knot tight and straightened. "You may just be smarter than you look, Hawthorne."

He chuckled. "Good luck there. Although, getting in with her friends sounds like a solid plan."

"Better than the one you have going with Lydia." I stood and hooked the strap of my duffle bag over my arm. "How many times has she turned you down now? Five?"

The star quarterback shook his head. "I thought fame was supposed to bring the women to us, not drive the ones we want away."

I clapped him on the biceps. "Preaching to the choir, man."

"Good luck with your girl." Grant moved along to Saunderson, inviting him out to celebrate.

I was supposed to meet Amanda and her friends at one of my favorite hole-in-the-wall restaurants. The place was famous among the locals while remaining off the radar of the hordes of tourists that flocked to Southern California in the winter in search of sunshine and balmier weather. The owners were the sweetest people, and customers lined up for their handmade tortillas and authentic street-style tacos. My mouth watered in anticipation of juicy carne asada wrapped in a warm corn tortilla.

I pulled into a rare free spot on the street near the restaurant, then walked the block to the corner building. The scents of cumin and cilantro mingled with lime and ancho peppers hit me as I opened the front door. Amanda waved to me from a corner table near the back, and I made my way over to the group. Everyone was coupled up except Amanda, who sat near an empty chair, and Betsy, who stood with a Styrofoam container in a plastic bag.

"Are you not staying to eat with us?" I asked, eyeing her to-go bag.

"The best chips and salsa on the planet couldn't convince me to sit and endure a night of watching my best friends make fools of themselves in the name of love."

"What if we promise to behave?" Molly reached across the table to her.

Ben caressed Molly's neck with the back of his fingers. "Who's making a promise like that?"

Molly swatted at him while Betsy rolled her eyes.

"You can't help yourselves. It's fine. I have my salsa." She wiggled her bag. "And you guys can be as ridiculous as you want. Win-win."

"Sure we can't change your mind?" I pulled out a chair for her in case she would.

She shook her head. "Not even your bribery could get me to sit through a night of those two staring into each other's eyes." She motioned to Drew and Nicole.

"They did just get engaged," Jocelyn said blandly.

"I know." Betsy sighed as if a tragedy had occurred. She waved. "Have fun without me."

We watched her retreating back a few seconds before Drew broke the silence with a grin. "I'm going to have so much fun teasing her when she finds someone who makes her trip all over that sharp tongue of hers."

"I don't know," Amanda said. "I don't think Betsy is looking for love."

Jocelyn threaded her fingers with Malachi's. "When you're not looking for it seems to be the time love sneaks up on you, don't you think?"

I laid my arm along the back of Amanda's chair. "And when you find it, you pursue it with singular focus, knowing you're unwilling to go back to living without it."

The occupants around the table looked between Amanda and me. Just then, a server came to take our order, cutting off any further discussion. When she left to put our requests into the computer, I picked up the conversation and tossed the proverbial ball to Drew and Nicole. "That was some proposal. I have a feeling people are talking about it tonight more than the game itself."

Drew stared into Nicole's eyes. "I'll never forget how you looked standing out on that field. I should be upset you asked me first, but I don't even care. I just want to spend the rest of my life with you."

"You're welcome," Molly crowed smugly.

Jocelyn hid a laugh behind a cough.

"What?" Molly splayed her hands. "If it weren't for Ben and me, Nicole and Drew would never have had to spend time together. A fact I was reminded of in annoyed tones often enough not that long ago."

"They didn't like each other all that much at first," Amanda informed me.

"That's not exactly true." Drew held up a finger. "I always like Nicole. I just *especially* liked pushing her buttons and getting a rise out of her."

"He used to say all sorts of things to rile her up." Ben chuckled. "Remember the time you argued for more offshore drilling sites?"

Nicole groaned. "He'd take any position, even if he didn't believe what he was saying, just to oppose me on a particular point."

Drew kissed the tip of her nose. "She's so adorable when her eyes flash and her cheeks turn pink. I couldn't get enough of her passion."

They kissed, and I turned my gaze away to give them a modicum of privacy. "What about you two?" I asked Malachi, who seemed embarrassed by the public display of affection happening beside him. "What's your story?"

Malachi cleared his throat and wrapped his arm around Jocelyn's shoulders. "This little filly showed up at my ranch with her coworkers for a corporate retreat. I was an awkward, bumbling, tongue-tied idiot around her, but she had mercy on me anyway."

Jocelyn laid her head on his shoulder. "That's not how I remember it."

"That's because you're too good to me, darlin'." He nuzzled the side of her head with his nose.

The server approached with a steaming tray of

food. "Be careful," she warned as she placed our entrees in front of us. "The plates are hot."

"I don't think I've heard how you and Amanda met," Ben said around a mouthful of grilled fish.

Amanda waved her spoon in the air. "No one wants to hear about that."

"I do," Nicole said.

Jocelyn agreed. "Me too."

Amanda lowered her spoon into her Spanish rice and shoveled a bite into her mouth. She shrugged as she chewed, pretending to be too polite to talk with her mouth full.

I, however, had only squeezed the juice of a lime wedge over my tacos and had yet to take a bite. "It was after a game. We'd just been handed our backsides in a devastating loss, and the morale of the whole team was in the mud pits. Some of the other players' girlfriends were trying to cheer us up by pointing out the handful of good plays made and saying things like we'd get them next time and the season wasn't over. You know, stuff like that."

"Was Amanda one of those girlfriends?" Ben asked.

I rolled up a taco. "She was in the group, but she wasn't dating any of the players at the time. Anyway, she walked up to me and planted her hand on her hips, glaring."

"Uh-oh," Molly whispered with a smile on her lips.

"She said, 'If you'd lower your shoulder and stop acting like you're afraid of your own shadow, maybe you'd make it through the offensive line once in a while.' Then she proceeded to lay out every play like she was my coach and not even an ounce impressed with my performance."

Amanda took a drink of her water. "In my defense, you played horribly that day."

"Then she stalked off, leaving me with my mouth hanging open, wondering who the beautiful woman who spoke sports like an ESPN commentator was and how I could impress her enough to give me a chance."

"Which you did." Molly rested her chin in her hands.

I rubbed my shoulder remembering the injury I'd sustained. "Wasn't easy."

Drew jutted his chin at Amanda with a wry twist to his mouth. "What did you make him do?"

Amanda's gaze slid over to me, the memory of her challenge lighting her eyes. "I told him I'd go out with him if he got four sacks in his next game."

"Four sacks is a lot," Malachi commented. "Were you able to do it?"

"I made five." Because I knew then what was still true—I'd do anything for Amanda Murphy to give me a chance to prove myself and my love.

@PeterReynolds

The tacos at @LaMesa are the best in SoCal! #MomAndPopBusinessOwners

17

AMANDA

*M*y stomach growled like a lion waking up from a nap. I put a hand over my tummy and looked down at my middle. "Shh. You'll wake Delores."

Talking to my internal organs about an invisible disorder I'd named myself. Maybe I should give that psychiatrist that Stella kept recommending a call. Clearly, I was going cuckoo for Cocoa Puffs.

Oh! Cocoa Puffs. My inner six-year-old sat up at attention. Cereal for dinner could work. Maybe not the most balanced meal, but I hated cooking for just myself. One, I wasn't a very good cook. Two, it was impossible to find a recipe that didn't make enough food to feed an army. And since my skills in the kitchen were deplorable, that meant ending up with days of leftovers I didn't even want to eat.

I got up and made my way to the little corner

pantry in the kitchen. My gaze lowered past the one-minute rice and the instant potatoes and the just-add-protein meal-in-a-box thingies to the cereal on the bottom shelf. Then I remembered. In a moment of idiocy—probably after an impassioned speech from Nicole about eating to live instead of living to eat—I'd tossed out my sugary cereals and replaced them with healthier, fiber-filled options. No more Cocoa Puffs to turn my milk into rich chocolaty goodness. Goodbye marshmallows in the shapes of rainbows and four-leaf clovers. Hello tasteless wheat that reminded me of chewing on wicker furniture.

The corner of my lip turned up in disgust as I reached for the box. Then again, Tony's pizzeria down the street made a mean calzone. I'd be stimulating the economy and supporting a small business if I ordered takeout.

The fact I ordered from Tony's enough to single-handedly pay for his son's braces shouldn't factor into this decision. Oh, who was I kidding? There wasn't a decision to make. Cardboard swimming in milk, or a warm, melty, tangy pillow filled with cheese and tomato sauce. Yeah, not even a question.

I reached for my phone as a loud knock sounded from the front door.

Who could that be? A week ago, the only person at my door would have been the maintenance man whenever I had an issue with the sink not draining properly. The number of people who'd been in my apartment had multiplied exponentially. (I think that's how you use that math phrase?)

I opened the door, blinking in surprise at the figure before me. Peter, with shopping bags hanging from his hands.

"What are you doing here?" I wracked my brain but couldn't remember anything that indicated I should have expected his presence. Maybe he needed help with his social media accounts? But that wouldn't explain the groceries, and really, he could have just called.

Peter chuckled in an *aren't you cute when you're confused* type of way. How did I know the deep rumbling in his chest conveyed that sentiment? Probably the same way I knew he would breeze right past me in a second without waiting to be invited in.

Which he did.

Peter turned his hips and ducked his head a bit as he stepped over the threshold and into my apartment. He strolled into the kitchen and set the reusable canvas bags on the counter. As if he'd done the same thing a thousand times. As if he belonged there. In my kitchen. In my space.

"Peter," I huffed, letting annoyance tinge my tone.

Let him think the irritation was at him showing up unannounced and barging in. Assuming I didn't have plans, which I could've had. Better for him to think that than the truth: that my exasperation was with myself. Because I *wasn't* annoyed that Peter had just shown up. I *wasn't* angry that he looked at home pulling ingredients from his bags as if this—him here with me—were routine. No, my temper roared at myself. My weak will. I knew pushing him away would be the best thing for him, but I wanted to drag him close, bury my nose in the corner where his neck met his shoulder, and breathe in his scent.

Peter's long lashes lifted, and he settled his hazel gaze on me. "Amanda." His voice was deep and a little gravelly but full of patience and a hint of something else. Iron, maybe?

Well, I could be resolved too. "Peter, you need to—"

"Eat. I know." He nodded and shoved his hand back into one of the bags. "I'm starved."

I shook my head and folded my arms across my stomach, giving myself a little hug. I still stood near the door, and Peter was all the way in the kitchen. I should show some courage and walk over there. Prove to Peter I wasn't afraid of the effect he had on me...that he didn't have any effect on me at all.

But he did and I was, so I hugged myself tighter. "That's not what—"

"You like minestrone soup, right?" he interrupted again, pulling out a bag of carrots followed by a stalk of celery.

"Peter."

Something in my tone made him pause, press the palms of his hands to the counter, and lean forward, drilling his gaze into mine. The ring around his iris darkened. "My house is quiet, Amanda. Empty and silent, and I couldn't stand it anymore. Now, if you really can't abide my presence, then I'll pack all this up and leave, but I'd like to stay. I'd like to cook you a nice meal, and I'd like for us to eat together."

His mouth closed, but his eyes stayed focused on mine. The decision was up to me. He'd said he'd leave. My lips parted. I knew what I had to do.

"Peter…" My voice quavered. Peter's shoulders sagged, and he reached for an onion to put back in the bag. "Minestrone soup sounds delicious, especially on such a rainy day."

Coward! I couldn't tell if the voice in my head was mine or Delores's, which gave me a jolt.

"I heard on the radio we're supposed to get almost two years' worth of rainfall over the next week." Peter opened one of the lower cabinets. "Where do you keep your cutting board?"

I directed him to the cabinet by the oven. "In Southern California, two years' worth of rain is, what, four inches of precipitation?"

He laughed. "Something like that. Although I admit to not hating the cooler weather it's brought."

The heat kicked on just then, pushing hot air through the vents in the ceiling.

Peter smiled at me. "Still like the thermostat set at seventy-seven I see."

I shrugged. "Delores starts having conniptions if I get too cold."

Peter and I both froze, my words hanging in the air. I never talked about Delores. Not with anyone except my doctors, and then I rattled off symptoms in hopes *they'd* give *me* a name. The name of a real disease with a cure, or at least medications that could help manage the symptoms. Otherwise her name didn't normally pass my lips—not unlike an aversion to saying Beetlejuice three times. And yet, without thought, I'd shared that the cold triggered an adverse physical response in my body.

Belying his massive size, Peter took small steps toward the living room, watching me as he moved as if I were a scared bunny. Which, given how my heart raced, wasn't a bad assessment.

He dragged the crocheted throw off the back of the couch. As he walked toward me, I found myself trapped in his gaze, little bunny that I was. He wrapped the blanket around my shoulders like a cape, holding it together under my chin. "Well, let's keep you warm then," he said huskily.

All I could do was nod in response. Not a single part of my body felt cold in that moment. In fact, the opposite was true. I was in danger of spontaneously combusting. Warmth flooded my veins and set my skin on fire.

Peter stepped back, and in his place a rush of oxygen filled my lungs, reminding me how to breathe. I took a steadying inhale and wrapped the blanket around me like a cocoon. Another fitting analogy, as my insides now felt like the goo caterpillars became inside their chrysalides. Was it worth it? This tearing down of one thing to be built into another? Was it really worth the pain to be able to experience the joy of flying?

Hot oil popped and sizzled as Peter set diced onions to sauté. He added carrots, zucchini, and garlic that he'd cut into chunks or minced, then stirred the contents. The smell coming from the kitchen pulled me forward until I found myself leaning over the pot to inhale the fragrance. Peter added vegetable broth, tomatoes, and some canned beans he'd rinsed in the colander in the sink. A pinch of this seasoning and a dash of that. My kitchen smelled better than it had since I'd moved in.

"Where did you learn how to cook?"

He glanced at me as he stirred the soup with a wooden spoon. "It wasn't until I came to stay at Boys to Men that I knew what a home-cooked meal tasted like. Not one where an essential ingredient was love, anyway. John insisted on family dinners, no matter how much pushback we gave him by saying that we weren't family." His mouth pulled into a wry grin, and I imagined he was remembering some of the trouble he and the other boys had been.

"It took time, but it was over those meals together and the love and patience John poured into them and us that we began to realize family is more than the people who share your DNA. Family is the people who invest in you, care about you, love you, and walk beside you day after day, no matter what." He stopped stirring and looked at me, a sheepish grin tugging at his lips. "I guess that was a long way to say that John taught me how to cook."

I stepped back until my hip hit the counter. "I'd like to meet John someday."

I'd never really had a filter for the things I said, but the little control I did have had either completely left me or was trying to find its way through the brain fog between my ears. What other reason was there for saying these things I'd never intended to voice out loud?

Peter turned fully toward me, his gaze intent.

I would've retreated farther, but the kitchen counter hemmed me in. Settling the heels of my palms on the edge of the cold surface, I hoisted myself up to sit on the fake granite top, affording myself a few more inches of space from Peter. Needing a distraction, I peered into one of the canvas bags he'd brought. Something lay at the bottom.

"What's this?" I asked as I pulled out some sort of electronic device.

"I can't believe I almost forgot that. It's for you."

"What is it?" I turned it over in my hand. An MP3 player?

"Let's say it's the twenty-first century equivalent of a mixed tape."

I turned it on and thumbed through the songs that had been downloaded. "Roar" by Katy Perry. "I Get Knocked Down/Tubthumping" by Chumbawamba. "Fight Song" by Rachel Platten. "We Are The Champions" by Queen. "Eye of the Tiger" by Survivor. Further down, the tone of the songs seemed to change. "I Am Not Alone" by Kari Jobe. "Beauty For Ashes" by Crystal Lewis. "Overcomer" by Mandisa. "Rescuer" by Rend Collective.

I looked up at Peter, tiny pinpricks hitting behind my eyes. "I don't understand."

He took the MP3 player out of my hand. "You said you didn't have a fight song, so I thought you could borrow mine and a few others. I wasn't sure which one would speak to you. If Delores is being a nuisance and you want to go a few rounds with her, you could blast one of the songs in the top category. When you're feeling like you've been in the fight too long and you want to give up, a song in the second selection might help lift your spirits."

A lump lodged in my throat. "I don't know what to say."

Peter scrolled through the songs and tapped on the screen. A second later, the first notes of Tubthumping streamed through the speakers. Peter bobbed his head. "Just say you'll get back up." He wiggled his eyebrows and grabbed a carrot lying by the cutting board. He brought the vegetable up to his mouth like a microphone, then added his voice to the one-hit-wonder

British band repeating the same two-phrase lyrics with annoying frequency.

I giggled and held up my hand. "Not that one. I can't believe that's basically all there is to the song."

He grinned and turned off the song. "Ready to admit "Eye of the Tiger" is the ultimate fight song?"

"Not ultimate, but better than that one."

"Let's see." Peter scrolled again. "Maybe you'll like this one better. A little on the nose, but…"

He clicked and Rachel Platten's voice filled the kitchen. With the carrot still as a microphone, Peter pitched his voice to sound as feminine as possible and sang along to the lyrics of "Fight Song." I pulled my phone out of my pocket and started recording his antics, smiling so wide my cheeks hurt. He added a shoulder shimmy during the chorus, shook his finger when she sang "don't really care," then did some awkward ballet moves when the song slowed. The music picked up beat, and he shimmied his hips and turned in a tight circle.

Laughter beat at my chest for release, but I didn't want to ruin the video. Later I could relive this moment with something more vivid than my memory. When I was alone again, or when Delores was being a particular pest.

When Peter would no longer be here himself.

Peter shook his rear end, then did some sort of spin for his grand finale, striking a pose with his carrot.

Unable to be held captive any longer, my laughter bubbled free.

Peter's eyes glinted in victory, then landed on the phone in my hand. "That little song and dance number were for your eyes and ears only."

I wiggled my phone to tease him. "You mean you don't want me to upload it to all your fans?"

He growled. "No."

I made my thumb do an upward motion on the screen so he'd think I was swiping into a social media app.

He grinned then lunged forward, his right hip knocking into my knee, his body settling between my legs as I sat on the counter. My position brought us eye level, but I twisted away, giggling, and held the phone behind me and to the side. He leaned even further, crowding my space, so I put a hand on his chest and pushed. He didn't budge even a tiny fraction of an inch, the scoundrel. Not that my laughter was helping matters either, but playing keep-away had never been so fun.

I hooked my hand behind my back and reached as far as I could. My mistake came when I looked up. Peter's gaze narrowed. His pupils dilated. My laughter died in my throat. All of a sudden, I became hyper-aware of how little space there was between us. The insides of my knees pressed against his hips. His heart thrummed under my palm. Our breaths mingled together.

Peter's gaze dropped to my mouth. My lips felt so heavy under his direct gaze that they parted.

A strangled sound tore from Peter. Before I knew what was happening, his hand cupped my jaw, his long fingers curled into the base of my skull, and his lips crashed down on mine. His kiss was hungry with need, and I felt at once consumed by him.

There was nothing gentle or soft about him. He was demanding, the pressure of his fingers pulling me even closer. As if he couldn't get enough of me. As if he were afraid I'd vanish if he slowed or became more pliant. As if he were trying to pour five years of passion, frustration, and unrequited love into a single kiss.

In that moment, I knew that I had broken this man. When all I had wanted to do was let him soar by releasing him from my tether, I'd broken him.

And here he was, offering me his heart once again.

The phone clattered to the counter as I tenderly placed my hands against Peter's cheeks. I pulled back slightly, just enough so our mouths weren't a crush of pressure, then kissed him again, sealing a wound. Softly, my lips molded to his. Gently, they moved in a languid dance, each touch reassuring. Each caress a plea for forgiveness.

Warm liquid seeped into the pad of my thumb. I pulled back, but Peter wouldn't have it. In place of our lips, he pressed our foreheads together, our noses grazing. I looked up, and sure enough, a tear track traced over his cheek bone.

I was undone. Humbled.

I placed tiny kisses along the wet line.

"Amanda," he rasped. "I need you."

Three small words, but they seemed to be the key to unlocking so many desires.

I need you...by my side.

I need you...to stay.

I need you...to not push me away again.

I need you...to need me too.

With the tenderest of touches, I kissed the corner of his mouth. "I'm not going anywhere."

@AmandaMurphy

My word of advice for the day: if you love someone, don't set them free. Hold them close and never let go.

*E*very reflex in my body jolted and then immediately relaxed at Amanda's softly spoken *I'm not going anywhere.* We had so much to talk about. I needed her to know that I was here for her for the long haul. That Delores, no matter how much havoc she may try to wreak, couldn't and *wouldn't* make me leave Amanda's side. That was what teammates, partners, and especially those in romantic relationships did. I needed her to know she didn't get to choose for me. I needed to hear her reassurance that she'd never try to take that decision away from me again.

So much to say...

The sweet smell of her breath fanned over my lips.

...in a moment.

Sliding my hands to the small of her back, I pulled her close until she sat at the edge of the counter. Until the front of her body was flush with mine. There had been too much space between us for too long. I didn't want anything to separate us now. Not even air. I gentled my touch, afraid the hot need pouring like molten steel down my limbs would solidify and harden, hurting her with the strength of my passion.

My head dipped to hers, this time savoring the feel of our mingling lips. The sweet taste of Amanda. The feel of her in my arms.

As a foster kid, I'd never had a person. No mom or dad or aunt or uncle. No one to call my own. To claim. No one, until Amanda Murphy. If home was where your heart resided, then my home was with this crazy woman right in front of me.

I tilted her head to better angle her soft lips and deepen the kiss. I didn't want there to be any question. I was staking my claim and hoping she'd do the same. I'd searched for a home, for love, for so long. I couldn't believe what a precious gift I held in my hands.

Amanda's legs squeezed at my waist. Her chest pressed against mine with each shallow breath. A part of my brain urged me to hit the throttle, but years of self-restraint allowed me to pump the brakes. Take a step back.

Literally.

I looked at Amanda perched on the counter. Her lips were a full, amorous shade of pink—the evidence of my ardent attention. Her hair, which had been pulled up in a ponytail, was in disarray. The elastic had slipped down her silky strands and sat at a jaunty angle instead of squarely at the crown of her head. She looked wondrously and devilishly disheveled.

I curled my fingers into my palms so I wouldn't reach for her again. The sound of bubbling on the stove rescued me. I pulled my gaze away from Amanda and inspected our forgotten pot of soup.

"Hungry?" I pushed the question through my tight throat. It would take a minute for my body to obey my mind and calm down.

"Ravenous." Amanda's voice dripped with flirtation.

That wouldn't help. "Amanda." I tried—and failed—to sound disapproving.

She giggled, but a note pitched wrong. Turning from the stove, I studied her again. She didn't appear as relaxed as before. A stiffness had settled in her spine. Then I remembered she only said shocking things when she was hurting. When she wanted to divert attention away from herself and her pain.

I stepped closer but didn't touch her, not knowing where Delores worked. "Did I hurt you?" I'd never touch her again if that were the case. I'd love her from a safe distance. I'd—

Amanda reached out her hand, and I took it gently. "You didn't hurt me."

My gaze bore into hers, searching for even a hint of untruth.

Her fingers squeezed mine. "You didn't. In fact, when we were kissing, I felt…good."

My lips pushed into a slow, lazy grin.

She laughed and swatted my arm. "Go ahead and be smug, but I mean…" She shook her head. "You know how long it's been since I've felt good? Not just *not bad* but actually really felt good? When we kissed it was like…" Her eyes shone, and she shook her head again. "I don't know. Maybe all the happy endorphins in my brain momentarily drowned Delores until I could no longer feel her." Amanda's features softened. "All I felt was you, Peter."

I tapped my finger on the counter, forcing my body to relax instead of jumping over the line and tackling Amanda. If I had my way, the time for that would come, but it wasn't now. After a deep inhale through my nose, I looked up at Amanda and smirked. "So, what I'm hearing is I should spend the rest of my life kissing you. Done."

She laughed but shifted her weight on the counter.

That wiped the smile off my face. "You're hurting now though. What can I do to help?"

Her face flushed as if she were embarrassed. "The counter is a bit hard and cold. I should move to the couch." She scooted forward to hop down.

One long stride and I stood before her, right where I'd been not long ago. Her eyes widened in surprise as my arm swooped around her back and pulled her until she straddled my waist. I carried her to the couch and set her gently on the cushions.

The pink on her cheeks deepened. "I could have walked you know."

"But what would be the fun in that?" I winked.

She rolled her eyes, and I went back to the kitchen to ladle soup into bowls. Amanda had lain down while I was gone, but she sat up and put her feet on the ground when I walked over with food.

I handed her a warm bowl filled with soup. "Be right back."

Her apartment was small, so it didn't take any time at all to find her bedroom. Her bed had been made, covered with a sheer white spread with tiny buttons creating tufts here and there. Instead of a mass of small throw pillows that served no purpose, two large rectangular pillows rested against a wrought iron headboard. My practical, amazing woman.

I grabbed the pillows and turned to retreat from her bedroom, but my gaze snagged on framed photos lining a chest of drawers. Amanda smiled in a few of them, but her hair was shorter, like it'd been when we were back in college. The tight-knit people around her had her brown hair and startling blue eyes. A family photo then. Some of the other pictures had the same people, but Amanda was conspicuously absent from them.

"What are you doing?" Amanda called from the living room.

The muscles in my forehead released my furrowed brow as I stepped out of the bedroom and rejoined her.

She eyed the pillows. "What are those for?"

I fluffed the down and set the pillow against the

arm of the couch. "There. You can lean against those and still stretch out the length of the sofa."

She scooted until she was comfortable. "Now you don't have anywhere to sit."

"Au contraire." I grabbed my bowl of soup, lifted her feet off the end of the sofa, sat, and resettled her feet on my lap.

Her mouth dropped open, the soles of her feet sliding against my thighs as she pulled them away.

I grabbed both of her ankles in one of my hands. "Leave them, Amanda." Our eyes locked. The moment she recognized I wouldn't let her win this battle, her calves relaxed, and she crossed her ankles over my legs.

She brought the spoon up to her mouth. "If you want my disgusting feet touching you while you eat, I guess that's your choice."

I'd have to lift my hand off her shin to take a bite, but food could wait. Instead, I massaged her calf with my thumb. "That's right. *My* choice. And I choose you." My thumb moved in small circles. "Also, there's no part of you I find disgusting, and certainly no part I wouldn't want touching me."

Her face flamed, and she ducked her head to peer into her bowl. We ate in relative quiet, enjoying each other's company. I snuck small touches between bites. A kneading motion to the arch of her foot. Playing *This Little Piggie* with her toes. I was a starved man who'd been invited back to the table, and I just couldn't get enough of her.

Amanda's spoon clattered against the bottom of her bowl.

"Do you want some more?"

She put a hand over her middle. "It was really good, but I'm so full I couldn't eat another bite."

I took our bowls into the kitchen and rinsed them at the sink before putting them in the dishwasher. I'd let the pot of soup cool more before finding a container to store the leftovers in. I found a dishcloth and wiped down the counters, loading the cutting board and knife I'd used into the dishwasher as well.

Strains of music drifted in from the living room, lyrics from Isaiah 61 filtering through the space.

He has sent me to bind up the brokenhearted, to proclaim freedom for the captives and release from darkness for the prisoners, to proclaim the year of the Lord's favor and the day of vengeance of our God, to comfort all who mourn, and provide for those who grieve in Zion—to bestow on them a crown of beauty instead of ashes, the oil of joy instead of mourning, and a garment of praise instead of a spirit of despair. They will be called oaks of righteousness, a planting of the Lord for the display of his splendor.

Amanda listened to a song from the second section of the downloads on the MP3 player. My heart swelled. Maybe the music would help her in a way she wouldn't allow people to.

One section of the verse repeated in my mind—a crown of beauty instead of ashes. Amanda believed she was as worthless as a pile of burnt and crumbling wood, but I saw the true beauty within her. The kind that rivaled any royalty.

I jerked open drawers in the kitchen, searching for anything that could be fashioned into a crown. Maybe it was silly, and maybe I should just go out and buy her a real tiara, but I didn't want this moment to pass without some physical reminder for her to look at herself through my eyes. To remember God could make even ashes and mourning beautiful and joyous.

A pad of sticky notes lay on the counter by the wall. The top piece of paper had the beginnings of a grocery list on it. Bread, eggs, cheese. I tore off the top memo and pressed it to the counter, then peeled off about ten more. Taking the shears from the knife block, I made horizontal cuts in half of the papers. Without tape, my makeshift crown wouldn't last long. Then again, nothing lasted long with paper as building material. But it would do.

For now.

I used the sticky strips on the memo squares to build a line and pattern of uncut then cut pieces—tall then short—then bent that line until it created a circlet. Hmm. A bit small, but it should be able to perch on Amanda's head.

Careful not to crush the delicate crown, I walked back into the living room with my offering. All that was missing was the velvet pillow to transport my crown jewels.

Amanda saw me walk in, then eyed my arts and crafts coronation piece. She snorted. "What is that?"

I knelt before her like a humble servant would, hamming it up so I could hear her laugh again. "This, your majesty"—the paper chain wobbled in my hands as I lifted it to her head—"is your reminder that no matter how ugly or hard or despondent Delores makes your life, God can take that and transform it into a crown of beauty, oil of joy, and garment of praise." I settled the memo pad circlet on top of her head.

Amanda's fingers rose to cover her mouth. Her eyes shone. "Oh, Peter."

I placed a soft kiss on her lips, then took my place at the end of the sofa with her feet.

She scooped up her phone from the coffee table, then held it slightly away from her face. She sent me a small, abashed smile. "I wanted to see how it looked but didn't feel like getting up. Selfie mode on the camera works great as a mirror."

I chuckled. "You might want to go ahead and take a picture. That thing's going to crumble like a blitzed quarterback any second. A strong wind could break it."

Her smile widened, then she shifted her gaze to her phone and took a picture. "I won't need a photo to remember your sweetness, but you're right. I doubt I'll be able to preserve your creation for long." Her fingertips brushed the side of the crown, then her smile slipped by degrees until she practically frowned. "Peter."

I pressed my thumb over the ball of her foot. "Hmm?"

"I'm sorry."

My hand froze.

"For hurting you five years ago. I thought I was doing the best thing for you." She visibly swallowed. "I thought you'd be better off without me."

Anger, fierce and sudden, rose from my gut. My fingers twitched. If I could take that thought of hers into a dark alley and pummel it to pieces, I would. It deserved to die and never be resurrected.

I reached over and cupped Amanda's cheek. Captured her gaze so she'd hear every word about to pour from my heart. "The best thing that has *ever* happened to me is you. Never *ever* doubt that, do you hear me?"

She blinked fast, as if to hold back tears, and nodded.

"Good. Now that we have that settled..." I pulled out my phone and unlocked the screen.

"What are you doing?"

I tapped into an app. "How does the saying go? It's not official until it's Facebook official? Now that I have you back, I want the whole world to know it." I tilted my head until my face paralleled the ceiling then I shouted to the universe, "Amanda Murphy is my girl-friend again!"

She leaned forward, laughing as she covered my

mouth with her hand. "Shh. My neighbors are going to complain."

I kissed her palm. "I don't care. I'll shout it from the rooftops."

She picked up her phone and pointed at mine. "I think we'll tell more people this way and won't get the cops called out on us."

After we changed our relationship statuses across all our social media platforms, our phones started blowing up with notifications. We turned off our devices so we wouldn't get interrupted. I had years of missing Amanda to make up for (and *cough* make-out with!) after all.

@PeterReynolds is now in a relationship with @AmandaMurphy

3.8k Likes 1.2k Comments 648 Shares

19

AMANDA

"Murphy. In my office. Now." My boss, Jim, stuck his head in my tiny cubicle long enough to issue the command, then vanished. He didn't wait to see if I'd follow, knowing my little feet would scurry in his wake like a fish on a line.

He walked around his desk when we entered the privacy of the four walls of his office, turning the leather chair so he could sit. "Close the door," he said without looking up.

The door clicked shut behind me. Was I in trouble? The last time one of my supervisors had looked so serious, I'd been transferred to Jim's division here with the Condors. Had Jim not been satisfied with my work? Was I going to get fired?

"Take a seat, Amanda." He indicated a chair across the desk from him.

My stomach plummeted as I lowered myself onto

the cushion. I crossed my legs and hooked my hands around my knees.

Finally, Jim looked up. He leaned back in his chair and crossed his arms. "I need to know. Is this all some kind of publicity stunt, or is it real?"

This? It? "Is what real, sir?"

He straightened. "You and Peter Reynolds. Your relationship status. Are you and Peter really dating, or is it some type of ruse to keep him trending? My wife assures me a fake public relationship with an athlete to help him with the press in some way is the plot of a number of romance novels she's read."

I almost laughed that his question had been spurred on by his wife's reading habits. My humor died, however, when the thought of potentially losing my job reentered my mind. I'd never paid attention to any policies about office romances or dating within the franchise. Admitting Peter and I had rekindled the spark between us might cost me my place here.

I pictured myself gathering my belongings for a second time and exiting the building for good. I'd practically lived and breathed sports media for the last few years. When I couldn't deal with Delores and my own life, I'd escape into stats and focus on building up the public opinion of an athlete. Some had received more sponsors or garnered farther-reaching opportunities because of my hand online.

I waited for the dread to pool in my stomach at the potential loss of employment.

And waited.

Nothing.

Instead, all I could think about was Peter and his ever-changing eyes. How he'd carried me to the couch, then handcrafted that flimsy, wonderful crown. How he'd literally kissed my pain away.

I could always find another job, but I could never replace Peter.

I lifted my chin. "Peter and I are in a romantic relationship. If that means you have to let me go—"

"Let you go?" His bushy eyebrows jumped. "Why would I let you go? Granted, I'm not going to give you all the credit, as the boys have worked hard on the gridiron this year, but we haven't received this much positive publicity in nearly a decade."

Oh. "So dating isn't against policy?"

Jim snorted. "Everyone here is an adult. As long as you're not breaking any laws and your behavior doesn't reflect poorly on the franchise, we couldn't give two crackers what you do on your personal time."

"Then...why..."

"Predicting and directing the public's opinion is my job. I just needed to know which direction this thing was headed so I could stay on top of any potential roadblocks or collisions." He wiggled his mouse to wake up his desktop computer, then settled his hands in front of the keyboard. "Now, when can we schedule an interview with one of the journalists? They've already been calling in hopes of an exclusive."

"Interview?" I squeaked. I'd done lots of interviews, but I'd been the one asking the questions, not answering them.

Jim glanced away from his computer screen. "Of course. You're the Condors' equivalent to Princess Diana. A homegrown, obscure nobody landing football royalty. Fans are used to seeing supermodels and actresses on players' arms, not a Midwest small-town girl who's better with computers than she is with people."

Jim told it like he saw it. He didn't mean to be offensive.

I mumbled something about talking it over with Peter, then stumbled to my six square feet of office real estate. I logged into my computer and quickly opened enough browser windows to pull up every personal social media page.

The notification numbers made my eyes bug out in cartoon proportions. I'd tripled my followers overnight, many of those people leaving comments on a picture I'd been tagged in by Peter.

Blood rushed in my ears as I stared at the photo. Molly had to have taken the picture the night of the gala, but it wasn't one in my phone's camera roll. Peter stood next to me, smoking hot in his tailored tux. But instead of looking at whoever was taking the picture, he stared down at me with an expression that could only be described as wonder. That *too good to be true, can't believe my eyes* sense of awe. As if I took his breath away.

My lungs released with a woosh. Looking at him looking at me took *my* breath away. How could I have been so blind and stupid as to push him away all those years ago? How much time I'd wasted and pain I'd caused simply because I thought I knew better. Because I'd let Delores have too much power in my life. Let her become a voice so loud she drowned out my own. No more. I was going to take back the driver's seat of my life. And the more people in my lane, the better.

Maybe it was the influence of Peter's updated version of a mixed tape. The language of music still beat in my soul, but the lyrics of Lesley Gore's "You Don't Own Me" pulsed in my mind, and I silently belted the words out in a personal serenade to Delores. From this moment forward, I was breaking free of the prison she'd made of my body. I wouldn't allow her to tell me what to say or what to do anymore. And I'd no longer use her as an excuse to shut people out of my life who had done nothing but love and support me. People like Peter and my sewing girls.

Picking up my phone, I opened a group text.

Amanda: Emergency lunch date needed. Are you guys available to mee at the Pie Shop at 12:30?

Nicole: I have the day off, so I can be there.

Molly: Emergency? Are you okay? Do you need someone now? Ben's mom can watch Chloe. Where are you? I'm coming now!

Amanda: Calm down. Maybe emergency was a

poor word choice. I just have something I need to tell you all.

Betsy: Good news or bad news? Will I need earplugs to drown out all the squealing or should I prepare to deliver a right hook to a certain football player?

Jocelyn: FaceTime me in please!

Amanda: @Betsy. Neither of those so...neutral news? @Jocelyn. If Malachi weren't so good to you, I'd be angry at him for taking you away from us.

Betsy: I guess I can get away.

Molly: I'll be there.

I clicked out of the app and laid my phone on my desk. I had actual work to do, but I couldn't seem to tear my gaze away from the picture Peter had posted. Directing the cursor to the comments button, I clicked and watched the words of thousands of people load. Most were encouraging and wished both Peter and me well. Some were trolls who needed to learn that if they didn't have anything nice to say, they shouldn't say anything at all. If I wasn't going to let Delores have a say anymore, I certainly wasn't going to expend any energy on some haters neither Peter nor I knew.

Speaking of Peter...I missed him, which was silly because he'd stayed at my apartment until late the night before. In fact, I'd practically been falling asleep with my head in his lap. (While the foot massage had been great, his fingers in my hair felt even better. Plus, the position made it convenient for him to lean down or for me to push up and steal some kisses.) After he'd chuckled and said I was starting to snore—which I promptly and vehemently denied—he'd kissed me goodnight so we could both get some sleep. That had only been a few short hours ago. How unprofessional would it be to sneak down to the training field then drag him to a supply closet to continue making up for lost time?

The thought was a fun one, but fearing for my job once in the day had been enough. Instead, I grabbed a piece of paper out of the printer, then retrieved a marker from the drawer in my desk. I wrote out a note in big letters—**Thinking of you**. I held the paper at chest level while angling my phone for optimal selfie advantage, then snapped a picture, sending the image to Peter.

He was probably busy either in the gym or in one of his many meetings, so I hadn't expected my phone to vibrate in my hand almost instantly.

Peter: This is the best thing I've seen all day. You're gorgeous.

Pretty sure I had bags under my eyes from the few hours of sleep I'd managed, plus I'd forgotten to set my alarm, so hadn't taken a shower. Just as well, since Delores liked water as much as the Wicked Witch of the West. Some dry shampoo and a side braid were about all I'd been able to do in the time I'd had to get my bedhead in some sort of order.

Gorgeous wouldn't have been the word I'd have used to describe myself.

Peter: Are you free for dinner?

Dinner made me think of Peter in my kitchen, which made me think of the firm pressure of his lips on mine, his strong fingers tangled in my hair as he held my head in place and devoured my mouth like a starving man.

I swallowed and tapped out a yes, glad I didn't have to say the word out loud, as it would've come out breathless and weak.

Peter: Great. I'll pick you up at 5:30.

I spent the rest of the morning scheduling posts for the week on the Condor's official pages. When time for lunch rolled around, I gathered my keys and drove down to the bay to the small restaurant near the water's edge that made the best savory and sweet pies around. Nicole's car with her *Save the chubby unicorn* bumper sticker was already parked in one of the spaces farthest from the entrance. I smiled as I parked next to her. She may be exhausting at times with all her soap boxes, but she had a heart of gold. Taking the farthest spot and walking so that others who have more difficulty with mobility could park closer was just one of the simple ways she made a conscious effort to think of others first on a daily basis.

The smell of buttery, flaky crusts welcomed me into the Pie Shop like the outstretched arms of a Southern granny.

All three of my friends had beaten me and resided at a table near the glass case showcasing the restaurant's dessert pies. Lattice-crust tops, torched meringues, fresh fruit on tarts with a shiny glaze. If I weren't so nervous about confessing to my friends, my mouth would be watering in anticipation.

Betsy spotted me first, one corner of her mouth pulling down as she studied me walking toward them. I could practically see her mind working to figure out why I'd gathered them all together. Especially since we'd get together in a few days for our weekly sewing time. Although, even Molly and Nicole, the only two left in the group who actually knew how to sew, did less and less work with the Singer every week.

Molly had rows of lines creasing her forehead, her aquamarine eyes large as she looked at me with concern.

When I reached the table, I fell into the last empty seat like I'd trekked the Sahara Desert, not simply walked from my car to the chair. Each and every joint throbbed with a bone-deep ache, and fatigue weighed me down. From lack of sleep—yes. Because Delores sapped my energy and left me in a constant state of tiredness and pain—also yes. But even more from the weight of the deceit I'd been carrying around instead of letting my friends help me shoulder the burden.

I opened my mouth, but Nicole held up her hand. A second later, a server approached from behind me. My friends ordered first, since they'd perused the menu while waiting for me. When the server turned to me with his pen poised, I asked for the chicken pot pie. I needed the comfort only butter and cream could bring.

Nicole held up her hand again. "Let me get Jocelyn on the phone before you start." After a few rings, Jocelyn's face filled Nicole's phone screen. Nicole propped her phone up against the napkin holder at the end of the table. "Okay, now you can tell us what your emergency is."

"Well, it's not really an emergency, per se."

Betsy huffed. "Quit stalling and spit it out."

"I've been lying to you." The words rushed out, and I covered my face with my hands. I couldn't bear to see the looks on their faces.

"What do you mean lying?" Molly asked. Her voice sounded small. Out of all my friends, Molly would be hurt the most by my words and actions because of her strict truth-telling policy that seemed more of a compulsion stemming from childhood issues. My keeping things a secret and not being honest must be a punch to her triggers.

"Fibbing, being disingenuous, deceitful, false, duplicitous." Betsy spoke to Molly but hadn't taken her eyes off me. Every word felt like a stab, and I winced. "You're a teacher. I'm sure you could come up with a few more synonyms."

"Maybe not so helpful, Bets." Jocelyn's voice came through the phone's speaker. Her gaze swung to me. "What have you been lying about, Amanda?"

I rubbed at my temples. Headache or not, Delores wouldn't stop me from finally telling my friends the truth. "You know when you all showed up at my house unannounced for your little intervention?"

"About why you kept canceling plans?" Nicole clarified.

"Yeah."

"Wait. You and Peter aren't back together? But I saw the Facebook status. And the way he looked at you and couldn't keep his hands to himself. That was a lie? You guys aren't dating?" Molly's bottom lip pushed out, something she'd picked up from her four-year-old stepdaughter.

"We are dating," I assured her. Then added, "Now. We weren't that night."

"You used him as an excuse to cover something else up," Betsy stated matter-of-factly.

I took a deep breath in. "Yes. Because, see, I've been hiding a secret."

"Shocking." Sarcasm coated Betsy's whisper.

"What is it, Amanda?" Molly reached over and covered my hand with hers. "Whatever it is, you can tell us."

My gaze swept over my friends, then in one motion, I gathered all my words and shoved them out of my mouth. "I have an invisible disease, some sort of autoimmune disorder. The doctors don't know which one exactly, and so I've named it Delores, and she makes me tired all the time. I ache all over, and sometimes I'm in too much pain to do much of anything, and that's why I've had to cancel on you so often, and I'm so sorry for lying, but my family thinks nothing is wrong with me and I'm crazy and it's all in my head, and I couldn't stand for you guys to think that too, so Delores became my little secret that I never told anyone, but that was wrong, and I'm telling you now, and I hope you can forgive me and that we can still be friends." I slammed my jaw shut and stared down at the table.

Quiet followed my confession, my friends so silent that I could make out the conversations going on at other tables.

The family behind me made plans to check out the tide pools at Cabrillo National Monument at Point Loma while another couple discussed her parents' upcoming visit.

Had I rendered every one of my friends speechless? Even Betsy?

"Okay, first things first." Jocelyn sounded like the supervisor she used to be at the financial conglomerate. "There's nothing you could do that would make us stop loving you or being your friend."

"Speak for yourself."

I blinked at Betsy while everyone else glared.

"What? All I'm saying is that if she turns out to be some kind of female Jack the Ripper, I'm not going to just hold her hand and skip down the street."

At that, tension melted.

Nicole grinned. "Have you ever skipped down a street in your life?"

Betsy nodded. "Once for PE in elementary school. It was awful."

Molly smiled at Betsy, then turned her gaze on me. "We don't think you're crazy, and I'm sorry your family hasn't been more supportive."

"But we're all practically adopted sisters now, so we'll stand in their place for you, right girls?" Nicole softly slapped the table.

"Right," they all answered.

Nicole tapped her chin. "Have you tried an anti-inflammatory diet? You know, the foods we eat can heal or harm our bodies."

"What about a Lyme test?" Molly asked, her eyes bright. "Ben was just saying the other day that lots of people aren't getting the help they need because insurance companies are tying their hands on testing for Lyme."

"Slow your roll, guys." Jocelyn laughed. "Let's *support* Amanda. Not overwhelm her with possible unwanted advice or questions."

"I have a question." Betsy raised her hand.

"Bets, I just said—"

"If you and Peter hadn't fixed whatever broke you up in the first place— Wait. It was this ridiculous business, wasn't it?" She waved her hand like whatever my response would be wouldn't matter. "What changed?"

I shrugged. "I finally stopped denying what I'd

always known: I simply don't want to live without him."

@Dani55

I want a man to look at me the way @PeterReynolds looks at Amanda Murphy.

20

PETER

I unbuttoned the cuff of my sleeves and rolled the length up my forearms. Unseasonably warm weather had pushed pause on winter for a couple of days, but the forecast would dip again soon. The temperature could be close to eighty degrees one week, then down to the fifties the next. Pretty soon the nearby mountains would be welcoming in snow, and thousands of people would momentarily trade in their surfboards for sleds and rubber tubes. SoCal, one of the only places you could bum on both the sunny beach and the snowy mountains in under two hours.

I reached across the truck's console and grabbed the plushie of a California Condor wearing a team jersey, sitting in the passenger seat. Maybe I should've stuck with a traditional bouquet of flowers, but I'd seen this guy in the pro shop and felt compelled to buy him for Amanda. He wasn't necessarily cute—Condors were

vultures after all, with bald heads and skinny necks—
but there was something about him that made me
smile. I hoped Amanda would agree.

Pocketing my keys, I left the truck and made my
way to the entrance of her apartment building. Dinner
seemed pivotal, in a way, yet all I felt was a deep sense
of relief instead of nervousness—like someone who'd
been holding their breath for a long time and had
finally been able to release a long exhale.

Technically, taking Amanda to a Boys to Men
dinner wasn't the same as taking her home to meet my
family. We'd have to drive out to the correctional
facility where my mom was serving yet another
sentence. As for my dad... who knew. The two humans
who'd given me life may've been tied to me by DNA,
but they'd done nothing to deserve the title of parents.
Only one man had loved me like a father, and that was
John. He'd had a hand in molding me into the man I'd
become, and I wanted him to meet the woman who
held my tomorrows.

I knocked on the door, then held the soft stuffed
animal up to my face so he'd be the first thing Amanda
saw when she opened the door. A second later, the
mechanisms in the lock sounded and the door opened.

"Aww. He's so cute."

Funny how people's voices changed when their
sentences started with *aww.* Kind of soft and smooshy,
the vowels making their lips pucker.

My gaze dropped immediately to Amanda's mouth.

Sure enough, her lips were pursed, basically begging to be kissed. Who was I to deny her? I lowered my head and captured the slight pout, delight filling me when her arms snaked behind my neck in response. Nothing in my life had ever felt as right as holding Amanda in my arms.

We finally, slowly, broke apart, and her slightly unfocused gaze returned to the cotton-filled toy in my hands. I held it out to her. "Something for you to snuggle up with when I'm not around."

She took the condor and hugged it close, her head tilting to rest on the fuzzy bald head as she rubbed her cheek against the softness.

I grinned. "I think you missed the part about it being for when I'm *not* around."

She tossed me a saucy smile but deleted the space between us and slipped her arms around my waist, squeezing like a blood pressure cuff.

Chuckles rumbled in my chest as I wrapped her in my arms. She rested her cheek against my heart, and the echo of my pulse sounded in my ears. I breathed in deep, needing to savor the moment with all of my senses. Her hair smelled lightly of citrus. Her skin was warm and soft.

Amanda leaned back and stared up into my face. We'd spent hours talking since that kiss in her kitchen. Apologies had been made as well as reassurances. But there was something that still needed to be said.

I brushed aside a wayward strand of hair and trailed

my fingers down her temple to her jaw. "I never stopped loving you." My voice came out raw, years of bottled-up truth—the disuse of the declaration—scraping against my throat. "I love you still."

Her blue eyes misted, and her throat worked as she swallowed. "I don't deserve you," she whispered.

I wanted to crush her to me, constrict my arms until she was held firm in my embrace. But I didn't want to hurt her. I'd never want to hurt her. So instead, I gathered her tenderly. Gently. If not for the lump at the base of my throat, I'd mention how grace and love went hand in hand. How none of us had received what we truly deserved. Not from God, anyway. Then I'd make a lame joke and say it was *I* who didn't deserve *her*, but we could spend the rest of our lives trying to deserve each other.

She tilted her chin up, and I peered into her beautiful face.

"I love you too, Peter. I wish—"

My finger against her pillowy lips stopped her speech. "I know, but we won't let the shadow of regrets steal the brightness of our future."

She kissed my finger, then smiled. "That was beautiful. I'd forgotten how well you did in that creative writing class Freshmen year."

I brushed more hair away from her face. "Only when you're my muse."

She snuggled deeper against me, and I held her a few moments longer. As much as it pained me to move from our position, I let my arms slide from her back. "We should get going if we don't want to be really late."

Amanda locked her door behind us. "Where are we going? And better yet, am I dressed appropriately?" She stopped and looked down at her outfit.

My gaze traveled over her. I reminded myself to focus on her clothing and not how the black leggings she wore hugged the curve of her calves or the way the light-weight sweater dress rounded over her hips. I cleared my throat, pulse drumming in my ears. "You are perfection."

Her cheeks pinkened.

There she was. My Amanda. Not the girl with a mouth fit for picking up guys at a bar scene, but the one who flushed at a simple, sincere word of praise.

I reached for her hand and threaded our fingers together. "And we're going to family dinner at Boys to Men. You said you wanted to meet John." I paused, rethinking my plan. "But if you'd rather go to a restaurant, that's fine too. Just let me call John…" With my free hand, I slipped my phone out of my pocket.

Amanda laughed, reached across my body, and covered my hand with her own. "Don't do that. I'd love to meet John and see the place you called home for so long."

"Okay then." I pocketed my phone and squeezed her hand.

By the time we made it to Boys to Men, the last serving platter had been set on the table. John met us at the door with a huge smile and even bigger hug. He beamed at Amanda, welcoming her in to the bungalow that had seen better days. "I'm so happy to finally meet you, my dear."

"It's nice to meet you too." Amanda turned to me, eyebrows raised. "Finally?"

John chuckled. "Oh yes. Peter has been talking about you for years. Not always in the best of terms, but I knew that would only be a matter of time. When a man is haunted by a woman the way Peter was by you, well, that just means there's unfinished business." He waved a hand. "Poor analogy, and I don't believe in ghosts or anything, but I think you get what I'm saying."

I grinned and threw my arm around Amanda's shoulders. "Come on, Casper."

She shook her head at me and let me lead her to the dining room. I introduced her to all the guys.

"You're the one in the TikTok video with Peter." She pointed to Trey.

Trey's chest puffed. "Someone had to make it look good."

Miguel slapped Trey's stomach, causing him to expel air with an oomph and curl forward. "Making the video look good was my department."

"This is Miguel," I said to Amanda. "He filmed and edited. Easy peasy stuff since he's a tech genius."

Miguel ducked his head.

"Oh yeah? I work on computers all day but still have IT on speed dial. What aspect is your favorite?"

He scratched behind his ear. "Umm, I like coding."

Trey snorted. "Bruh, that's just code for hacking."

Miguel pushed Trey's arm, then Trey pushed him back.

John laughed. "Okay, I think the food is getting cold." He offered grace for the meal, and the boys descended on the platters like a pack of wolves on a carcass.

"So," Amanda said around a bite of tuna noodle casserole, a twinkle in her eye as she turned to John. "I bet you have loads of stories of Peter when he was younger."

I groaned. "No need to dig up ancient history."

She smirked at me. "You get off scot-free when it comes to embarrassing baby pictures. My mom has an album filled with photos of when I hated diapers and found every which way to peel them off—even when she used duct tape."

John wiped his mouth with a napkin and stood, smiling.

"John," I warned. I knew exactly where he was headed. He kept a bookcase filled with albums of all the boys he'd helped raise. He gave each of us a similar book when we moved on from living under his roof.

Mason snickered behind a forkful of noodles.

I speared him a look I'd give an offensive lineman. "Laugh it up, chuckles. Your turn will come."

Mason shoved the bite of food in his mouth, unperturbed by his future embarrassment in the name of John's pride.

John returned holding a black leather album. He opened the plastic pages and set the book in front of Amanda. "Here's Peter the night of the high-school sophomore dance."

I didn't have to look at the picture to know which one John pointed at. I hadn't wanted to go to the dance in the first place but had been wrangled into it by a teammate. I'd scowled at the camera, determined everyone should share in my misery. I'd already grown like a beanstalk, towering over the backup kicker standing next to me. I'd reached six feet tall before my fifteenth birthday, and the teal suit John had helped me find at a local thrift store only drew attention to the fact I was all arms and legs. Add to that some unfortunate acne, and there I stood in all my awkward teenage glory.

Amanda hid her smile behind a hand as she gazed down at my photo. She turned the page then laughed outright.

"Do I even want to know?" I hung my head.

"Bruh, I've seen those pics. There are no good ones." Trey smirked.

John chuckled. "The donation we got from the church group."

Oh yes. Everything in the bag had been second hand and at least six inches too short.

"You were adorable." Amanda looked up at me, smiling with a softness that touched hidden corners in my heart.

"Somehow I doubt that's what the headlines would say if a media outlet ever got their hands on one of those pictures," Trey teased.

"Keep talking and I'll add a few dozen reps of burpees to training this week and tell the guys they have you to thank for it."

Trey fluttered his lashes at me and pitched his voice higher to mimic a female. "You were adorable, Peter."

Amanda laughed, the sound brightening all the dark places created by my past. Sometimes a person didn't know what they'd been missing until they found it. But I knew. And I'd found it in her. I felt like I'd been waiting my whole life for Amanda, and now that she was mine again, I never wanted to let her go.

@PeterReynolds

We've talked about fight songs, but what about love ballads? Which song would you dedicate to your special someone?

21

AMANDA

*W*hy were doctor's offices always so cold? I'd waited enough hours within the clinically white walls covered with medical infographic posters to have learned to bring a cardigan, but even with my fuzzy sweater, my teeth threatened to clatter as I suppressed shivers. I hugged my arms against my stomach and hunched my shoulders, conserving body heat. My hand poked out of my one-man huddle, grasping my phone. The doctor was already twenty-five minutes late for my appointment, and who could say how long it would be until he finally showed up. His record for tardiness sat at fifty-seven minutes.

I looked down at my phone screen, my right thumb finishing tapping out a Twitter post. *See Jim? My job, in its essence, could be virtual. I could work from anywhere.*

Like the comfort of my own home. Maybe one day he'd see that.

I hit the blue Tweet button and watched the update pin to cyberspace. A bright graphic of burgundy and navy. Grant Hawthorne front and center with the football in his hands, flanked by his favorite wide receiver and the running back with the fourth highest rushing yards in the league. The text had been short and sweet.

@CondorsOfficial

#WildCardGame weekend. Don't miss the game
Saturday @ 3:00PST. #CondorsSoar

The Wild Card game kicked off the playoffs. The Condors, being the second-seeded division winner, would host the seventh-seeded team, the Wildcats. All the commentators predicted an easy win for the Condors. The team may've had a rocky start to the season, but the players had found their rhythm and were working together like a well-oiled machine now. Granted, there were always upsets in football, but all the odds favored the Condors for a victory and the chance to play again in the next round to fight for a spot in the Super Bowl.

If they lost…that was it. The end of the season for my favorite raptors.

Which was why I'd told Peter I didn't want to see

him until after the game. Not technically accurate. I did *want* to see him. But he needed to focus on annihilating the other team on Saturday. That took a lot of mental and physical preparation. I wouldn't allow myself to be a distraction and potentially bring the team down.

My lips tingled as I remembered how he'd tried to convince me to change my mind. When his words wouldn't move me, his lips had employed other methods to persuade me.

"That's not fair," I murmured against his mouth.

He kissed me again. "Neither is telling me not to see you every day."

I clucked my tongue. "A few days won't hurt you."

His nose nuzzled my cheek as his lips trailed to the sensitive spot below my ear. "I think you're killing me already."

The memory helped to warm me from the inside out. I clicked out of the Condors' official media accounts and logged into Facebook on my personal profile. Mindlessly, I scrolled through the feed, stopping to look at funny memes.

A soft knock sounded on the door before Dr. McGregor walked in. "Sorry to have kept you waiting."

I set my phone down and looked up at him. "It's no problem."

He pulled his rolling chair out from under the counter and sat down, then tapped away on the keyboard to bring my medical file up on the computer. "How have things been going?"

"Pretty much the same as usual." My gaze flicked to

the computer, but the screen was tilted away so I couldn't see the content displayed. "I'm really interested to know what the results were on that last test you ran though."

"Before we discuss that, let me take a look at you."

I'd been examined by doctors so many times I could answer all their routine questions before they'd even been asked. Even though it felt as if I'd recited the list a thousand times, I repeated the battery of symptoms Delores liked to set off like some maniacal engineer at a computer's mainframe.

Dr. McGregor's mouth pulled down as he removed his hands from checking the glands in my throat. He wore a familiar expression: forehead wrinkled, eyebrows drawn in. He looked like he'd just been given a test in a foreign language and he couldn't even decipher the questions, much less work out the answer.

I sighed, and my shoulders dropped a fraction of an inch. "Let me guess. The results of the test didn't help you to figure out what I have or how to treat it at all."

When I'd first come to see Dr. McGregor, he'd been confident he could figure Delores out and find a way to serve her an eviction notice. Or at the very least, hobble her so she couldn't wreak quite so much pain and control so much of my life. Even after the first few tests had come back with unexpected or inconclusive results, he hadn't given up, so I'd stayed hopeful as well. Every test and unsuccessful medication attempt had chipped away at my optimism. Now, as I waited to hear what I already knew he would say, I only felt numb.

"I'm sorry. I wish I had better news for you."

I nodded, dazed. Not what I'd wanted to hear, but at least the test eliminated a possible disorder. A dwindling of possible culprits had to mean we were getting closer to figuring out what Delores was and how to manage her, right?

I pulled my cardigan more snuggly around me. "So, what's next? Another test? A different medication to try?"

Dr. McGregor's head tilted to the side. His eyes softened with pity, causing my stomach to harden to a peach pit. "I've tried everything I know to try and have inquired of my colleagues as well. I'm sorry, but there's just not anything else we can do for you."

He kept talking. I knew because his lips were still moving. All I could hear, however, was the high-pitched ringing in my ears.

That was it? They couldn't help me? What was I supposed to do now? How could doctors not know what was wrong with me? I'd just have to live with the constant pain and fatigue? The fevers and chills and body aches? For the rest of my life?

My chest tightened as my neck flushed. The back of my eyes stung. I. Would. Not. Cry.

Somehow, I managed to thank Dr. McGregor, check out at the desk, and make my way back to my car. As soon as the heavy door shut behind me, the floodgates opened. My face crumpled as deep sobs wracked my shoulders. I clenched the steering wheel and laid my forehead on the back of my fingers.

All these years, everything I'd been through, and nothing. None of it had mattered. I was right where I'd started. Right where I'd always been.

A guttural cry wrenched from my throat.

Now what? my mind screamed.

I took a deep breath and let my head fall back. A tear squeezed out of the corner of my eye, trailed down my temple, and got lost in my hair.

Now what? I repeated the mental plea more quietly.

"I want to be at your appointment with you." Peter smoothed back the hair from my face, his hazel eyes changing from amber to green as he stared down at me.

"You can't. You'll be right in the middle of drills."

"I'll play hooky. I want to be there for you."

"You'll get in trouble and receive a huge fine, among other things."

"Worth it."

"Peter."

He sighed. "Fine. But even though I can't be there with you, remember that you're not alone. Never alone." He tapped my breastbone with two fingers. *"Because you always carry my love with you wherever you go."*

I took a deep breath through my nose and let it slowly out of my mouth, trying to calm myself and get back under control.

My phone pinged from my pocket. I wiped the

remaining tears from my face and fished the cell out of my jeans, opening the messaging app.

Nicole: Peter said you had a doctor's appointment today. How'd it go?

Molly: I've got chocolate! How many bags do we need? One to celebrate or two to drown our sorrows?

Jocelyn: If you need a mini vacay, let me know. You're always welcome at the ranch.

Betsy: Let us know if we need to start planning your funeral.

Molly: Betsy!!!

A strangled laugh pushed past the lump in my throat. Peter had been right. I wasn't isolated. My family may have turned their backs on me, but I had him and I had my girls. I'd thought I was strong enough to walk this journey by myself, and maybe I was, but I didn't have to find out. What a difference it made just knowing I wasn't alone.

Were there other people in the same position? Someone who didn't think another soul could possibly understand the struggles?

I glanced down at my phone.

Be authentic. You never know who you could inspire. The nudge in my mind came in the deeper tones of Peter's voice.

Before I could second guess myself, I snatched the cell and opened my favorite social media app. I turned the camera to selfie mode, then grimaced at my reflection. Bags puffed under my eyes, my fair skin was blotched from crying, and my nose resembled Rudolph's. Definitely not a put-together, her-life-is-perfect look. Then again, my life wasn't perfect. No one's was. And it was okay to be vulnerable.

I hit the button to make a live video and watched the green dot next to the camera light up.

"I'm going to apologize in advance, because I'm probably going to cry. I mean, I'll try not to, but I won't make any promises."

Little notices floated on the side of the screen to tell me people were watching.

"I wouldn't say I'm a really private person, considering so much of my life revolves around sharing bits and pieces of myself to social media. But I've always been conscious of what I share. Always the good news. The filtered pictures. That sort of thing. If I were an apple, I'd have only showed you the bright, shiny side, keeping the bruised and rotting portion of me in the shadows.

"You see, my life isn't really social media-post perfect." I forced a laugh, but all the while tears gathered in my eyes. "Shocker, right? And I wouldn't normally have even dreamed, much less been brave enough, to share this not-so-perfect part of my life if it weren't for a man who believed in me. Who stood in the corner for me even when I didn't think I needed anyone and pushed him away. I wouldn't be here, stripping away my veneer of *fine* to be authentic with you now. You see, maybe one of you can relate to my story.

Maybe one of you won't feel so alone, knowing there are other people struggling and battling with the same things. There is strength in that. In holding each other up. Holding each other's hands."

A tear slipped out. I lifted my hand and caught the liquid under my eye with the pad of my thumb. "I'm not even making sense, am I?"

Comments scrolled in from viewers, but I didn't allow myself to read them. To get distracted or derailed. My family would probably say this video was just me trying to get even more attention, but I couldn't let their voices silence mine. Not if I could reach across the void and help to lift someone else up out of the pit of hopelessness.

"You see, I'm sick. I'm sick with some sort of autoimmune disease, and the doctors don't know the cause or the name of my disease or how to treat me. I'm currently sitting in my car in front of the doctor's office. Not ten minutes ago, my physician basically said that there's nothing else he can do."

I looked away and took a calming breath. Even so, my vision swam. "So I'm left with all these questions, you know? Basically, questions like *what now*? And the sinking feeling of despair that there's no hope of getting better. That my life is going to be a constant battle against pain and health issues. I'm so mad that I want to hit something." I released a long breath. "While at the same time, I'm so tired of fighting that I want to give up."

I looked away again and gave my head a little shake. "This is the part where someone better than me, deeper than me, would say something profound and uplifting. I wish I had something like that, but I've got nothing." I hiccupped. "Just keeping it real. Anyway, yeah, if you're going through something similar and you feel alone or like no one understands and you need someone to talk to, I'm here. Obviously, I don't have all the answers." A self-deprecating snort escaped my mouth. "But I can be a listening ear."

I passed the phone to my other hand. "Well, I'm going to go home, put on a pair of yoga pants, and try to forget today even happened. I'll respond to your comments later when I'm in a better headspace. Until next time." I waved to the camera and ended the live recording. My shoulders sank, and I rested my forehead against the steering wheel, depleted.

Later, I'd pick myself up and dust myself off, but for now, I just wanted to curl up into a ball and ignore the world and all its harsh realities.

I drove home on autopilot. The numbness in my fingers made it difficult to unlock the door, but the deadbolt finally gave. I changed into a pair of yoga pants and a soft U of F sweatshirt, then crawled on top of my bed, my knees to my chest. The gut-deep, shoulder-shaking sobs had passed. In their wake, silent tears gathered then fell. My head pounded and an all-consuming ache settled in my chest. I imagined

Delores doing a victory lap, high-fiving all my over-achieving white blood cells.

Not sure how long I lay there not moving. Long enough to watch the light streaming through the blinds on my window crawl down the side of the far wall. A sound came from the front door and broke through the silence. The latch of the door turning. The sound of footsteps across the tile floor. Maybe I should be worried someone was in my home when I hadn't given anyone a key, but I couldn't muster up an ounce of energy to care.

I felt more than saw the presence standing in the doorway to my room. The hulking form made me squeeze my eyes shut against another wave of grief.

Peter didn't say anything as he walked in and approached the bed. My back was toward him, but I couldn't even make myself roll over. The bed dipped with his weight, and a second later, one arm slid underneath me, the other on top, and I was cocooned in the safety of his embrace. He pulled me back until his chest lay flush with my spine. His heat seeped into my frozen places, thawing me. The cadence of his heart beat a steady rhythm, my pulse seeming to synchronize with his.

After I'd soaked in enough of his strength, I managed to speak. "What are you doing here?" I reached up and covered his hands, hoping the action would convey that the question was asked not as an accusation. More like, *How'd you know I needed you?* And maybe, *Thank you for ignoring me when I said we shouldn't see each other until after the Wild Card game.*

"I saw the video. Only death could have kept me away." He pressed kisses into my hair. "I'm so proud of you. And I'm so sorry about the doctor. What can I do? What do you need from me?"

I pulled his arms more fully around me and used his body like a security blanket. "Just keep holding me."

His lips found the shell of my ear, and he whispered, "I'll never let you go."

22

@*F*ootballLeague

Kick off in 15 min. Who will win the #WildCardGame? Condors or Wildcats?

@Drake2

Time to eat some kitty carcasses. Too much? #CondorsBeatWildcats

@CondorsOfficial

Opening drive puts up 7 points! #CondorsSoar

@FootballLeague

Pratt to Forte plus the extra point ties the game. 7-7 #AllTiedUp

. . .

@FootballLeague

Pick 6! Pick 6! Watch this near impossible interception and forty-two yard run by Jeon to put the Wildcats
in the lead.

Watch #WildCardGame on CBS // NFL app //
Yahoo Sports

@CondorsOfficial

Let's go defense! #HoldTheLine

@FootballLeague

Pratt and Forte connect for their 9th post-season
touchdown.   #dynamicduo   #PuttingDownPoints
#GettingItDone

@TimButler

@Condors have plenty of time to come back and
win the game. It's not over yet. #StillMoreGameToPlay
#ComebackKings

@WesHughs

How was that pass interference? The ball was
uncatchable! #Blindrefs #LetThemPlay #CondorsSoar

.   .   .

@CondorsOfficial

Fifty-three-yard field goal is good! Thank you, Abeson!

@FootballLeague

Halftime score. Condors 10, Wildcats 21

@JoseRojas

Where have the @Condors gone? Looks like a different team playing. Hoping for a better second half from my guys.

@CondorsOfficial

That ball had wings! Hail Mary pass for sixty-six yards! Hawthorne shows off his guns!

@FootballLeague

Sack and fumble! Recovered by the Wildcats

@CondorsOfficial

Fourth quarter

.   .   .

@FootballLeague

That's game. Final score- Condors 10, Wildcats 34. Congratulations Wildcats. Always next year Condors. Stay tuned as the Steelers take on the Saints in New Orleans @ 6:00!

@GrantHawthorne

Thank you, Condors fans, for a great year. We'll come back stronger next season.

@BlakeSaunderson

Both the game and life are a process. We have to learn from the wins and the losses.

@PeterReynolds

Grateful for the opportunity to play. Grateful for fans and teammates and the support of my lady. Ultimately grateful for God from whom all blessings flow.

23

I'd been interviewed numerous times after and since the loss of the Wild Card game, and my public response never wavered. I wished we'd played more cohesively as a team. That we hadn't let nerves break our rhythm and miss key plays. I was disappointed the season ended in such a way, but we'd all work harder to make next year even better. I kept to myself how I thought the refs had made unbalanced calls. A simple count, which commentators were already pointing out, would show the weight of flags thrown on our team compared to the Wildcats.

But what I *really* wouldn't voice was how shallow my disappointment ran. It only sank to the depths of a game not well played. On every other front, I may've even felt a secret pool of relief. No more playoff games meant Amanda wouldn't try to distance herself so I could "focus" on the team and winning on Sunday.

Newsflash—didn't matter if she stood two feet or two hundred miles away; there wasn't a time when I didn't think about her.

Another benefit of Saturday's loss came from Amanda herself. (All the plusses of the game's outcome revolved around her.) Her concern over the blow of losing the game rallied her out of her own bad-news letdown. She'd spent the following three days trying to cheer me up. I may have laid on how affected I was a little thicker than called for, but I couldn't resist the extra attention. She turned me into a starved-for-affection puppy, and I was more than happy to soak up every little pet and coo she gave me.

I had no pride when it came to her.

The best product of no longer having any pressing commitments to the Condors was the time I could devote to planning the biggest and most important commitment of my life.

I opened the black velvet box in my hand and examined the ring inside for the thousandth time. I hadn't understood any of the terminology the jeweler had spouted. Things like D color and VS1 clarity. The only clarity I had came when I held the ring in my hand and knew it belonged on Amanda's finger. Tiny sparkly diamonds haloed a single circle stone like little petals of a delicate flower. Just like her name meant, she'd become my bliss and joy, and I planned on spending the rest of my days bringing those two emotions to her life.

This ring was the only one that mattered in my life at the moment. Let the other teams fight over a chance at Super Bowl rings. Amanda agreeing to marry me would make me happier than any Lombardi trophy could.

The lid of the box closed with a pop, and I buried the engagement ring deep in my pocket. Now to check to make sure the rest of the players were in position.

Peter: Everyone ready?

Betsy: Is all this really necessary?

Peter: Yes!

Molly: Don't worry about us. We'll be where we're supposed to be when we're supposed to be there.

With that assurance, I put my phone in my other pocket. I climbed out of my truck in front of Amanda's apartment building and took a deep breath. We'd made plans to spend some time at the beach. The temperature hadn't climbed to the point of bringing locals to lounge on the shores, so there was a good chance we'd have the beach relatively to ourselves. The rest of my plans for the day...well, hopefully they'd be a pleasant surprise.

Amanda opened the door before I even had a chance to knock, looking radiant in a pair of black jeans, a soft blue sweater that brought out the deeper color of her eyes, and a pair of brown boots that reached the bottom of her knees.

She stuck a foot out. "There are only a handful of

boot-wearing days here in SoCal. Gotta take advantage of each and every one of them."

I reached out and caressed the apple of her cheek.

"You look beautiful." My voice cracked at the end, thick with emotion. I loved this woman so much my chest felt inflated to the point it would burst. I needed to get myself under control or she'd suspect something was up and the surprise would be ruined. "Ready to go?"

She nodded, and I took the keys from her and locked the front door behind us. The moment I could, I grabbed her hand and laced our fingers together. One would think the more time we spent together, the more I got to touch her, the more my hunger for her would be satiated. But the opposite proved true. My appetite only grew. I doubted I'd ever have enough of Amanda.

"So, I'm curious. Are we watching the rest of the playoff games or boycotting football until the end of the season?"

We. Man, that sounded good. I'd waited so long for her to see us as a team, a united force. I leaned down and captured her mouth because I became powerless to do anything else. When I had to come up for air, I smiled into her eyes. "No need to boycott. We may be out, but I feel nothing but grateful. Football brought you back to me, after all."

She blushed, and I helped her climb into my truck. Her hand ran over the cloth seat. "I can't believe you still drive this girl. With just your signing bonus you could have upgraded a few times over."

I caressed the cold metal to the curve of the roof. "Too many good memories were had in this truck." I shot her a wicked grin. "You remember that time—"

She covered my mouth with her palm, her face flaming. "I remember." She grinned back at me and shook her head. "You're a very sentimental man, Peter Reynolds."

I pressed a kiss to the center of her palm, piercing her with the directness of my gaze. "Only when it comes to you." I shut her door before I succumbed to the temptation to kiss her again. If everything worked out and she answered my question how I hoped, I'd have the rest of my life to kiss her whenever I wanted.

Traffic was light as we made our way north. We drove in comfortable silence, content to hold hands on the middle console and listen to music on the radio.

Amanda whipped her head around. "Wasn't that our exit?" She pointed out the window behind us.

"We're going to a different beach."

"Oh."

I braced for more questions, but she seemed content with the simple explanation. Before long, we pulled into a small parking area off the side of the road in front of a long stretch of white sandy shore leading into the deep blue of the Pacific Ocean. Wetsuit-clad surfers bobbed in the water waiting for the perfect wave. To the right, bluffs jutted up from the soft ground, towering in layers of rock and sediment offering a breathtaking landscape...and corners in which to hide.

Amanda opened her door before I could round the hood and do it for her. She took a deep breath as soon as her feet hit the asphalt, filling her lungs with the briny ocean air. A light breeze played with tendrils of her hair, casting them out behind her like a veil.

I grabbed her hand again and led her to the beach, setting out a path to meander between the water's edge on one side and the rocky cliffs on the other. Her free hand crossed her body, and she clutched hold of my arm, almost hugging my limb to her chest. Looked like I wasn't the only one who couldn't get enough.

I chuckled and kissed the top of her head. Eyeing the shoreline, my gaze zeroed in on a point where the bluff stepped out an extra foot as if reaching for the sea.

My heart knocked against my ribs in a staccato rhythm. The moment I'd been waiting for. In five... four...three...two...

Jocelyn stepped out from behind the bluff, holding up a poster in front of her. Amanda sucked in a breath beside me, her body going rigid before she started to shake.

She read the large note card under her breath. "I knew that I loved you when you gave me pointers on how to improve my game."

Jocelyn beamed at us as we slowly walked past her.

"Peter," Amanda whispered on a breath. "What are you doing?" Emotion thickened her voice.

I squeezed her hand and continued to lead her forward. Betsy stepped out a moment later also holding a poster. Her normal blasé expression had been replaced by a genuine smile.

"When we are together, I understand the phrase 'coming home' for the first time." Amanda sniffed and leaned her head on my arm.

Nicole emerged next with another poster. She appeared on the verge of happy tears.

"You've owned my heart all these years, and I never want it back."

"Peter." Amanda hugged my arm.

It took everything in me to keep us moving forward.

Finally, Molly appeared, her grin huge as she held up her sign.

"You and me together forever—an unbeatable team."

I stepped in front of Amanda, halting her forward motion. She covered her mouth with her fingers, her eyes shining. My gaze bored into her, pouring all of my love into a single look. Without breaking the contact, I lowered to one knee in the sand and fished the velvet box out of my pocket, opening it and holding it up as an offering and representation of my heart.

"Amanda Murphy, I love you. For richer or poorer, I love you. In sickness and in health, I love you. Will you make me the happiest man on the planet and become my wife?"

"Yes!" she shouted before launching herself into my arms and tackling me to the ground. She framed my face and attacked my lips. I only too happily surrendered immediately.

Her friends surrounded us, offering congratulations. I sat up and helped Amanda to her feet.

"Let's see the ring!" Jocelyn made to grab Amanda's left hand.

Amanda's mouth formed a silent O as her eyes widened. "The ring! I didn't knock it into the sand, did I?"

I held up the box, the ring still safely inside. After prying the jewelry from its case, I slipped it onto her finger. She glowed as she stared at her adorned hand, her friends oohing and aahing.

I shifted on my feet, suddenly nervous. "Do you like it? We can exchange it if you don't."

She gaped at me. "Like it? I love it! It's gorgeous!" She wrapped her arms around my waist and squeezed, resting her head on my chest. Lifting her chin, she looked up at me. "Thank you for loving me despite Delores."

I kissed the tip of her nose. "There is no *despite*. I love all of you. Delores included."

She scrunched her nose, so I kissed it again.

"I mean it. I love all of you. I want to marry all of you."

She squeezed me tighter. "I want to marry all of you too. Beauty for ashes, right? We've gone through the ashes; now we can spend the rest of our lives relishing the beauty we make together."

A mental image popped into my mind of us creating love and beauty together. I growled and hugged her fiercely. "I like the sound of that."

@PeterReynolds

She said yes!

@GrantHawthorne

@PeterReynolds At least one of you got a ring. ;) Congrats man

@CondorsOfficial

Congratulations to defensive end Peter Reynolds on his engagement to Condors social media manager Amanda Murphy!

@AmandaMurphy

My life may not be perfect and at times I feel broken, but you make me whole. #ISaidYes #Engaged #ManOfMyDreams #ThisIsOnlyTheBeginning

THANK YOU!

Thank you for being a rockstar reader! If you enjoyed this story, I'd be thrilled if you left an honest review on Amazon and, while you're there, consider following me to receive alerts on new releases! Stalk away, please! And be sure to stop by www.sarahmonzonwrites.com/subscribe to sign up for my newsletter and receive a free novella!

God Bless,
    Sarah

ALSO BY SARAH MONZON

Made in the USA
Las Vegas, NV
16 June 2022

50334166R00146